THE WIDOW VERSES

also by ken levine

North of Nowhere

Before It Gets Dark

THE WIDOW Verses

ken levine

THE WIDOW VERSES
Copyright © 2020 Ken Levine

All rights reserved. No part of this book may be reproduced (except for inclusion in reviews), disseminated or utilized in any form or by any means, electronic or mechanical, including photocopying, recording, or in any information storage and retrieval system, or the Internet/World Wide Web without written permission from the author or publisher.

Book Cover and Interior Design by VMC Art & Design LLC

Published in the United States of America

ISBN: 979-8602993899

acknowledgements

When we think of British cinema many women of a certain age immediately come to mind. Helen Mirren. Dame Judi Dench. Maggie Smith. In literature British authors like Penelope Lively, Rosamunde Pilcher, and others routinely pen stories with older main characters. Anyone who has watched Downton Abbey can't help but notice that many of the main subplots revolve around the travails of people well into their seventies. In our youth obsessed culture most popular films and novels have no interest in anyone over thirty, much less over seventy. Thus, the idea was born for *The Widow Verses* to try and explore themes not often delved into by most American books and films. Here's hoping Marian's story sparks a few conversations about the intersection of age and renewal.

I continue to be blessed by compatriots who love literature and the process of making it come to life. Julia Scotton makes sure every word is believable and absorbing. Eric Gardner scours over every sentence with his expert scalpel and enriches every page. Nancy Green, Patricia Kaufman and Nancy Forden were particularly generous with their time and editing attention. Charles Detrizio, as always, offered great encouragement. Victoria Colotta of VMC Art and Design, as usual, created a striking and memorable cover and also made many keen suggestions to improve the manuscript. The novel is a far richer experience because of their involvement and I cannot thank them enough. Finally, my family (Daniela, Noah, Isabella, and Ethan) lets me play author between trips to the supermarket and the baseball diamond, among other things, so I am lucky to have their permission to pursue my passion.

1

marian

For some reason Marian thought the people who owned cemeteries would treat each grave as if it were sacred. In the end, she realized it was a business, like everything else. So, when she visited her husband's grave to bring fresh flowers every other Friday she didn't expect it would be perfectly manicured or at least not the way she felt it should have been. The hedges weren't crisply trimmed with sharp edges, and the grass was draped over the bottom of the gravestone so she couldn't make out the words. She thought about bringing her hedge clippers, but was afraid someone would see her and think she was a lunatic.

Today was no different. The grass was annoyingly long and a troublesome weed was trying to poke through. *A weed*. No, that was too much. She kneeled down and tugged it out by the roots and walked briskly to the main building. Avoiding the road, she underestimated the distance weaving mildly uphill through all those graves, and, by the time she made it to the building, she was breathing hard, which served to emphasize her frustration. There was a man behind the counter who was speaking in a near whisper to a man in a black suit with a shock of gray hair. Before she could stop herself, she had abruptly said, "excuse me," and when the man with gray hair turned, she could see he had tears in his eyes, which he quickly wiped away.

She felt something tap her shoe and realized some soil had dropped from the roots of the now-wilted weed. She felt ridiculous and petty.

"Yes?" the man behind the counter said impatiently. The man with the gray hair, who was obviously in mourning, waited for her to talk.

"It's...nothing. I can come back later."

"Fine." He went back to speaking with the man with the gray hair and Marian slinked away with the weed clutched in her hand. She shoved it into a garbage can as soon as she walked outside. Stopping to take a moment to gather herself, she noticed the man with the gray hair had followed her outside. He was greeted by a pretty young woman with curly black hair who said something to him and then buried her face in his shoulder. A little uncomfortable with the public show of grief, he pushed her off gently. They got into a long black limousine and drove in the direction of Marian's husband's plot.

Marian took her time walking back and without anything to obstruct her view, she watched the limousine meander through the virtually treeless cemetery. By the time she arrived at her husband's plot, it became apparent the man was burying someone— she assumed, his wife—about a hundred feet from her husband. She counted about twenty-five mourners gathered near an open grave and moved cautiously in their direction so she could hear what was being said. Leaning against a nearby tree, she could barely make out what the minister was saying but distinctly heard the word "she" in his remarks. A little girl who couldn't have been more than five or six looked over in her direction. *Wasn't she too young to be there?* Marian smiled at her, though the girl didn't smile back. It became clear that she was intruding once again and walked back, said goodbye to her husband, and returned to her car.

At her car, Marian looked for something to clean her dirty hands and found an old napkin in the glove compartment. When she finally started driving, she noticed the funeral had ended and the mourners were saying their goodbyes to each other. The road was so narrow (cemeteries were clearly not made for cars) that she had to wait for some cars to clear in front of her. She could see the man with the gray hair being hugged by some older women who were dabbing their eyes. He politely nodded as they talked. Then they hugged him again and walked away.

The cars finally cleared in front of her and she pivoted her foot from the brake and pressed the gas to cautiously move forward. When she passed the area near the funeral the man with the gray hair was walking alone, head down, to the limousine. He looked up, saw her, and nodded his head in acknowledgement. Marian wasn't sure if it was appropriate to smile so she just nodded back and kept driving. On her way home Marian decided she was going to call the cemetery to discuss its lackadaisical gardening efforts. It wasn't fair to her or the man or anyone else to visit an unkempt grave. Her mind wandered and she wondered how he would experience walking into his empty house after burying his wife. It was over a year since she had made that walk. Would he make it past the door a few feet before falling to the ground and weeping like she did? Would he scream how unfair it was into an empty house? Would he sleep the days away until day and night seemed to merge? She expected the transition to get easier over time, but there was no getting around the silence. No one else was there watching some blaring sports game on the TV or rooting around the kitchen calling her name because an item wasn't in the usual place. Marian never realized the absence of idle chatter in the house would be so jarring. You could get used to sleeping alone and the quiet of the night. However, the silence during waking hours, was unsettling and impossible to shake.

2

nathan

1971

There was drunk and then there was drunk, Marian thought to herself. She would have to use that line in one of her stories. The last cup of whatever it was they were all drinking had pushed her to a new level of inebriation. She tried to remember how she and her college friends had ended up sitting in this dank little apartment. It was lost on her at the moment. She tried to remember what day it was, but 1971 was as close as she could get to recalling her place in the universe right now.

There was a boy who was on the ratty brown couch across from her, and she was able to focus long enough to figure out he was smiling at her. She wasn't sure if she smiled back or even if she should, but before long, he walked over the table that separated them. She quickly leaned back because she thought he was about to jump on her.

"Long walk?" Marian asked sarcastically.

"I thought this was a more direct route."

He smiled and she noticed he had a gap between his front teeth as well as sweet dimples.

"What's your name?" he asked.

"That might be the only thing I do remember right now. Marian."

She stuck out her hand for some reason. She blamed her father for her ever present and sometimes too formal manners.

"I'm Nathan." He shook her hand and grinned. She liked those dimples.

"Luckily, Marian I remember where we are, despite the joint I just smoked."

"Can you fill me in?" Marian was struggling to keep her eyes open.

"My apartment actually."

Marian put her hand on his shoulder to steady herself and then quickly took it off. "Sorry."

"No problem."

"So, have you seen my friends? The people I came for. I mean with." She felt the alcohol start to come up on her.

"I don't know. They could be anywhere. It's a big house. You want to go home?"

"I think maybe I should."

"Where do you live?"

"Thompson Street."

"That's not too far. Let's go."

"Me and you?"

"I may be stoned, but I don't know if you can even walk."

Marian checked the state of her mobility by trying to get up, but she felt wobbly. Marian ordinarily would not have left without her friends, but there was something about Nathan that made her decide that she would throw caution to the wind.

"Can you help me up?"

Nathan pulled her up and she knew immediately that she was going to throw up. The only question was where. Nathan could see her distress and walked her to a bathroom and waited outside while she vomited. He leaned against the wall and closed his eyes and thought about randomness. His days at school seemed like a series of random events strung together, interrupted by classes. Tonight, he and his friends had gone to a party up the street where there wasn't anyone particularly interesting. But then here sitting on his own couch was an interesting girl who had wandered into his living room, and he was now waiting for her to finish vomiting to walk her home. She was a little waspy for his tastes, and she seemed a little uptight for someone so drunk, but he wanted to see where this random meeting would lead. Were they going to fuck? Kiss? Or just part and never see each other again? What would determine the outcome? A look? A comment? That must be the weed talking, he thought.

The door opened and he could see Marian trying to recover her dignity, as if she had just been powdering her nose. Though she forced a smile, he saw a pained look come over her face, and she retreated to the bathroom again. He was starting to tire of standing so he slid down to the floor and closed his eyes.

When Marian had finally finished in the bathroom, she was so embarrassed. Opening the door, she looked down to see Nathan sitting on the floor snoring. Relief washed over her. She wasn't going to wake him just to walk home with her. Luckily, she was feeling a little less wobbly now, so she walked straight out the front door, leaving him to sleep off his high. With a quick look back, Marian felt guilty that he was now slumped on the grimy floor, but she had to get out of there.

One of her friends was sitting on the curb with some boy lost in a long kiss that Marian thought might linger into 1972. She decided not to wait for her and kept walking. She set her eyes on the church perched on the hill overlooking the campus and used it as her North Star to guide her home. Her head was starting to pound again, so she tried to think of anything but her desire to wretch. Nathan's face lingered in her mind. He wasn't really her type. His whole look was a bit too *lived in* for her tastes. She tended to like boys with smart haircuts and crisp clothes, but she knew meeting one in 1971 was like trying to find a needle in a haystack. Even the Beatles had grown their hair out and had scraggly beards now. She preferred the pre-1965 Beatles' look. Meet the Beatles rather than Abbey Road.

She finally made it home to her dorm twenty minutes later and ripped off her clothes and threw them on the floor in her closet, away from her bed. She was never drinking again. Of course, she had told herself the same thing last week, but this time she really meant it.

3

condiments

Nathan slowly opened his eyes and saw what looked like a wall. His right shoulder ached and so he rolled on his back and realized that he was on the living room floor. The sun streaming in the window near the front door caused him to cover his eyes with his hand. He tried to recall how he ended up on the floor all night, but it was all a bit fuzzy. The last thing he remembered was that cute Waspy girl throwing up in the bathroom. Wasn't he going to walk her home? Where did she live again?

He pulled himself up and tried to clear the cobwebs from his brain. He was pretty sure it was Friday, which meant that he was unfortunately supposed to be working in the school cafeteria. The house cat, Nixon, was sleeping soundly at the foot of his bed. It didn't seem to matter how much he explained to Nixon that he wasn't a cat person. When they first found him sitting on the front porch Nixon only took a few days to decide that

Nathan was the weakling in the herd, who would break down and feed him. Nixon was sleeping on his bed by the end of the first week and there wasn't much he could do about it. At first, he was a little overwhelmed having to take care of an animal when he hadn't yet figured out how to take care of himself. As time went on though, he had to admit that it gave him some satisfaction that he could keep both of them alive.

Nathan plopped on the bed and Nixon stirred and crawled closer so Nathan would rub his belly. He only had about thirty minutes to get ready for work. *Marian.* Her name popped into his head. Even though she was inebriated and emptied the entire contents of her stomach into his toilet, she had a certain dignity that Nathan respected. Pluck was a word that came to mind, though he knew most girls wouldn't exactly be flattered by that description and might even be insulted. The college grounds were small enough that he figured he would eventually run into her. It used to bother him how tiny the campus felt the first time he visited with his parents. He thought it might suffocate him, but he had to admit his mother was right. She convinced him that he would be lost at some school where football stadiums and basketball arenas dominated campus life.

Befitting the campus, the cafeteria wasn't much bigger than the one in his high school, but the food was at least, edible. When he arrived at the admissions office with his father, the woman they met told his father many students worked in the cafeteria. It was all his father needed to hear. They marched over to the cafeteria and had him fill out an application. On the way, he heard how his father worked in the library stacking books and how that was a transformative experience in his education. He smiled and nodded his head, while wondering if parents really thought that their children believed half the malarkey they shoveled.

Nathan knocked on the back door of the cafeteria. The odor from the garbage piled in the dumpsters was particularly overwhelming this morning. It seemed like an eternity until one of the servers, who were mostly old women who barked rather than spoke, opened the door. There was a senior student coordinator who was in charge of meting out assignments. He was looking at a list when he noticed Nathan.

"You're late Hiller."

"Long night. Sorry."

"Well you're the last to arrive so you're on condiments."

"Really?"

Nathan hated the smell of all condiments. He always had. Whether it was ketchup, mustard, or even salad dressing, they disgusted him. He didn't know why. He had made that clear at the beginning when he was asked if he had any food allergies. He tried to pass his disgust off as a more sympathetic allergy. The manager didn't seem too impressed at the time.

Also, Nathan hated condiments duty because he might actually run into someone he knew. On the way to the back-storage room he was accosted by Claudia, which was a little awkward lately.

"Nate."

"No one else calls me that Claudia."

"Why not? It's cute. Like you."

"I have to get the condiments. Where are they keeping them now?"

"Oh, let me show you."

Claudia took him by the hand, like they were Romeo and Juliet or something. He never should have kissed her at that party a few weeks ago, but it seemed like the right thing to do at the time. Grain alcohol, even in small doses, was always troublesome. Claudia pointed him to the open boxes of ketchup and mustard. He thanked her, but not before she invited him to a party. He lied and told her he would come. He picked up as many bottles of ketchup as he could and walked to the condiment station in front of the cafeteria line. He was filling the containers when he felt a finger poke his shoulder. He turned and was shocked to see Marian.

"You're up early. Ever make it to bed?"

"Marian."

"You get points. For remembering."

"Of course, I would remember your name." Nathan said with as much conviction as he could muster. Now that she wasn't a shade of blue, she was prettier than he recalled. Her hair had fallen around her face and it was framing her delicate features and hazel eyes.

"So, you're the man to see if I want more ketchup, eh?"

Marian immediately wondered why she said things like that. She could hear her mother telling her not to make men feel inferior.

"That's me. Nathan the condiment man. So, you got home alright?"

"Yes, but I think I threw up a few more times. I kept my roommate, Hilary, up all night. Sorry about all that."

"Sorry I fell asleep on you."

"It's okay. It happens."

"You know I think we're having a party on Friday, if you want to come. You can bring whomever you want. Return to the scene of the crime."

Nathan smiled and she saw those dimples of his again and wanted to put her hand on his face. Was he being polite? Maybe he just wanted her to stop talking and leave him alone.

"Okay, I *do* know where you live. I think."

"Stetson."

"That's right."

"And you're..... Thompson?"

"Wow. That's right."

"Weird memory I have. Well, maybe I'll see you Friday."

"Hopefully, I'll see you then."

Marian walked away and she could sense him watching her. She wanted to turn around and confirm her suspicions, but she decided to let him have his moment. Her mother would have been proud of her.

4
feet

When Marian arrived home from the cemetery and walked in the door, she immediately remembered that she had forgotten to call the cleaning company. There was some chemical they were using that made her eyes burn and tear up. She didn't even want the help, but her daughter had insisted after she had sprained her wrist gardening. It was such a minor little thing she didn't know what all the fuss was all about. But her daughter seemed so concerned that she agreed rather than start a big kerfuffle.

She put her keys down on the table and realized her feet were aching. She kicked off her shoes and massaged her toes. She wasn't one to normally touch her feet, what with all the dirt and sweat they produced. She never understood how Nathan could feel comfortable massaging her feet. Not that she didn't enjoy it once it became clear she had no choice.

"Your feet are so far away from you, no one even thinks about them. They are clearly the neglected stepchildren of the human body."

When Nathan was baked, she usually was on the receiving end of his philosophical musings. He really seemed to want to massage her feet for some reason, so she let him do it. They had been dating for three months now and she was finally starting to get used to him placing his hands on her. Given that all of their nude couplings had taken place in the dark, he had to have figured out by now that she wasn't the most comfortable person with her body, but he never said anything to let on. They had been performing an exquisite minuet and Nathan was allowing her to lead. Marian figured he also had to know by now that she was probably a virgin, but he was lovely enough to avoid saying it out loud and embarrassing her. There was a moment early on when she almost told him, but then lost her nerve.

But now, with winter break coming, Marian was beginning to worry. Would he forget about her if they didn't make love soon? Maybe he had an old girlfriend back home that would try to win him back. She had never inquired about his former girlfriends, but given how much thought he had given to the human form, there had to have been many. Maybe his friends would laugh at him when he told them his new girlfriend was a virgin, and he would wonder if she was worth the trouble. As he rubbed her feet, she smiled at him and those dimples appeared. He seemed happy with her, but then again, not much seemed to bother him. She hoped there wasn't something going on inside

THE WIDOW *Verses*

that brain she was missing, because she found herself coming to rely upon him more with each passing day.

"I can't say I've given them that much thought, but I can see your point."

"I like how you humor me." Nathan crawled on his knees on the bed until he reached her face and he kissed her as she lay there.

"My mother would be proud of me."

"She doesn't think much of men, eh?"

Marian hadn't planned on revealing anything about her mother, but she couldn't help herself with him.

"She has her ideas, let's put it that way."

"That sounds like a challenge. When do I get to meet this complex creature?"

"Whenever you want to drive a thousand miles to my house."

"Don't think I won't do it. Does she listen to music?"

"Music?"

"Says a lot about someone. She into Sinatra? Probably not. Too East Coast. Elvis? Too wild, too hippy. Hmmmm. Ah. Big bands, right? Goodman?"

"Wrong."

"Oh yes. Classical. Am I right?"

"That would be yes."

"Should have said that first. Damn."

"So what does that tell you?"

"All I need to know."

"Oh yeah?"

"I'll have to wear my Beethoven smoking jacket then."

"A what?"

"You just wait and see. I'm dapper when I want to be."
"I'm scared."
"She'll love me. Just like you do."
Marian looked into his eyes to see if we was kidding or serious. She wasn't sure.
"Is that right?"
"You going to deny it?"
"Is that your way of saying something?"
"Maybe." Those dimples again.
"I would have just come right out and said it."
"You're the brave one. I see."
"I try to be."
"I know. And I do love you."
Marian knew he was serious because he didn't use those sorts of words loosely. She could barely breathe as her heart tried to catch up with her brain. She wanted to cry, but he might not understand her tears so she held back.
"I do too." She said barely above a whisper. He reached out and touched her face and caressed her cheek.
"I guess that settles that Marian Collingswood. Now what?"
Her head was swimming and she could barely concentrate on his words as he continued to caress her face. She closed her eyes for a few seconds and then opened them. When she opened them, he was wiping away a tear from one of her eyes that had formed without her realizing. She pulled herself up and, at the same time, pulled off her blouse. They would make love every night until winter break came and she would sit on the back porch of her mother's house in January and count the days until it was over. Her mother thought she was ill and kept feeling her forehead until one day toward the end of January when a

noisy car pulled up late in the night. Her mother awakened and looked out the window and saw her daughter bound down the porch steps and leap into some boy's arms. She nodded her head and looked for her housecoat. She surmised that her daughter's fever had disappeared.

5

baseball

Marian had been avoiding cleaning out Nathan's closet for more than a year and she wondered if he might not visit if his things were gone. She knew how insane that sounded, but so many of the thoughts that ran through her head these days seemed fantastic. Of course, the sheer clutter of it all was daunting, particularly for a neatnik like her. Over the years, she had tried to pare down his mess, but he would howl in protest when she told him what she was about to donate and toss. She usually relented, unless it was moldy or unsanitary in some other way. Even then, he would grumble. They were opposite in so many ways she often wondered how they had stayed together at all.

She opened the door and waited for something to happen. Other than startling a spider that scampered up the wall, there were no surprises. Marian put on her gloves and started pulling the closet apart and filled garbage bags labeled *junk* and boxes labeled *mementos* with Nathan's long forgotten possessions. However, there were a few items that vexed her. What to do with his baseball trophies? She didn't think her daughter would want them and, since she didn't know him in high school, she had no great sentimental attachment to them. She thought the whole idea of spending so much as an hour of your precious time watching the dreadfully glacial game of baseball was ridiculous. So, in the end, she decided they were junk and tossed them in a bag. His baseball cap was a different story. She picked up the red cap which was soiled so completely that it was more brown than red. She wanted to put it on, but it was so dirty she just couldn't bring herself to do it. She had actually considered burying him in his beloved Cardinals cap, but she thought it wasn't dignified.

⁓

"Stan Musial. Lou Brock. Bob Gibson. The Gashouse Gang!"

"The what?"

Marian couldn't understand why he insisted on wearing that ridiculous red cap.

"Dizzy and Paul. The Dean Brothers. They won 49 games in 1934. Nobody expected the Cards to win the World Series that year. The team was known as the Gashouse Gang."

"You clearly know too much about baseball."

They were hiking near her mother's house in one of Marian's favorite places. She wanted to share it with Nathan.

"Your father doesn't like sports at all?"

"He golfs. That's about it."

"Hmm. Golf. I know a little about golf. Not going to make for fascinating dinner conversation."

"You could actually talk about other things. You're a history major, remember?"

"Something tells me your father supports Nixon."

"He is a bit conservative. So current events *are* probably out. Didn't you take a course on the Roman Empire last semester? Can't you talk about aqueducts or gladiators or something?"

"If he's into aqueducts, I'm his man."

Nathan had been inching closer and now grabbed Marian by the waist and gently moved her against a thick tree and started kissing her.

"So that's your answer to everything? Making my brain into a puddle so I forget what I'm saying?"

"Seems to work."

Nathan shrugged and then kissed her again but Marian let herself go this time. His cap fell to the ground. Marian had always thought that making love outside was only for animals, but she probably wouldn't have resisted if he had given her that look of his. After a few minutes they separated and continued hiking until they had reached their destination. At the foot of a small mountain was the entrance to a cave that didn't look very inviting to Nathan.

"You think I'm going in there?" Nathan pointed to the cave.

"Are you claustrophobic?"

"A little. What's in there?"

"It's just a cave, but it's pretty cool."

Marian put out her hand for him to take it and against his better judgment he let her take him inside. It took a few minutes for his eyes adjust, but he was able to see that it wasn't as cramped as he expected. He kicked something and looked down to see that a beer bottle was skidding.

"It's a high school hangout." Marian confirmed.

"I see that. You spent some time here during your misbegotten youth?"

She could see he was fishing.

"Are you asking about past boyfriends?"

"You were a nun?"

"You were the first. Couldn't you tell?"

She was happy she could barely see his face.

"I don't know. I wasn't sure."

"Now you know."

"I'm honored."

They were still holding hands and she squeezed his hand in response.

They walked further into the cave and Marian remembered how her mother used to ask her why her clothes had a funny odor. The walls of the cave contained sulfur and when some boy would back her up her shirt absorbed its rotten egg smell. Her response was that she had been "hiking". She never inquired further but she had a feeling her mother was, as usual, already two steps ahead of her.

Her mother was waiting on the front porch reading when they arrived home. She looked up and her glasses fell to the ground. Nathan picked them and handed them back to her.

"Thank you, Nathan. Where did you two run off to?"

"Hiking," Marian said. Before she realized what she had said, her mother and her both started to laugh.

"I definitely missed something."

"Mother-daughter joke," Her mother explained.

"Ah. No more explanation needed."

"So you're a baseball fan I see. Cardinals."

Her mother pointed to his cap.

"That's right." Nathan was impressed.

"What do you know about baseball mother?" Marian asked.

"My grandfather was a baseball fan. I didn't have the heart to tell him I had no interest since he had no grandson to revel in sports with. He was a Cubs fan so, of course, he went on about the dreaded Redbirds."

"Very cool." Nathan said as he rearranged his cap and ran his hand through his hair.

"Who knew?" Marian said to no one in particular.

Marian had rarely heard her mother talk about her childhood. When she was younger she had imagined her perfect mother had been raised in an environment devoid of whimsy. So finding out that she had a working knowledge of something as frivolous as baseball was something of a minor revelation. Nathan had clearly disturbed the delicate balance that existed in their universe.

Marian was able to persuade her parents to let Nathan take her back to school in what her father called "that jalopy". It was going to be their first real road trip together and Marian didn't have the heart to tell him she got car sick. After about 100 miles her nausea got the best of her and she threw up in a gas station bathroom. When she walked outside Nathan was standing there.

"Are you…?"

"What? No. Just a little car sick."

"That sound brought back fond memories."

"Hah."

"You okay?"

"I get car sick sometimes."

"Why didn't you tell me?"

"I don't know. I thought you might leave me at my parents."
"Seriously?"
Nathan stopped by the car.
"Yes."
"Silly girl."
"We don't show any weakness in my family."
"I kind of got that. But their daughter's goofy boyfriend shows up out of the blue and they were perfectly sweet the whole time."
"Sweet?"
"Okay, not your Dad."

Marian nodded, opened the creaky car door, and put on her seat belt. Nathan got in, put his hand on her leg, and looked at her with that *everything is going to work out look* he had perfected. Sometimes she thought he was an old soul or she was dating someone decades older. She didn't tell him because he would have laughed at her and said something like: he hoped that meant he had gotten laid a lot. She rolled down the window, and Nathan unexpectedly took off his cap to put it on her head and explained that girls were sexy in baseball caps. She tried not to think of how old and smelly that cap looked because he was so pleased with himself. Marian figured that was as close to a crown as Nathan might bestow upon her for being his Queen.

6

perfect

1972

She was wearing one of those shear flimsy white frocks that Nathan would have invented, if they didn't already exist. It was summer and Marian was home despite her pleas to her parents to allow her to stay on campus. Nathan wondered if this wasn't a last-ditch attempt by her father or mother or both of them to detach her from him. Maybe he was just paranoid and they just wanted to spend the summer with their daughter, who would soon leave the nest and never return.

Whatever the reason, this summer he only had his friend Will, with whom he was staying in the same house they rented during the school year. He was planning on visiting Marian over the July 4th week, but she had called to tell him that her father was having some "elective surgery". That phrase always made him think that there was some vote held at the hospital among the doctors as to whether the surgery should be conducted ... all hands say, 'aye'. So, they planned instead on the first week of August after his class was over. Nathan was taking *The Robber Barons*, a short course about the industrialists who accumulated great wealth at the turn of the century. His professor made his opinion known early on that *Robber* was the proper adjective for these men who were at the vanguard of America's Industrial Revolution.

However, most of his free time was spent with Will. He was about six inches taller than Nathan and, it was clear that, when it came to women, those inches mattered. Will didn't go long without some conquest, but he never pressed Nathan to be a wingman or encourage him to cheat on Marian. Nathan knew that when he brought home two women that night he was probably thinking more about a ménage a trois then tempting Nathan. The girl with the shear frock peeled off for some reason and found her way to Nathan's room. Nathan was reading about Andrew Carnegie when she appeared in his doorway.

"Hey."

Nathan looked up and instantly saw *through* her blouse.

"Oh hey."

"Good book?"

"A little dry. You a friend of Will?"

"Oh, Will. Didn't know his name. We met tonight at Skelly's. One of my roommates is here too."

Here too. Interesting choice of words.

"You smoke?"

"I do." Nathan said a little too jauntily, he later thought.

She pulled a joint out of her pocket and Nathan reached

over behind his head and grabbed a lighter. She approached him and bent down and she caught him looking at her. Nathan knew there wasn't much longer to travel from here to there, and he wanted to tell her she needed to leave. But he didn't. A few hours later she was sleeping next to him, and he was trying to remember if he even knew her name. He decided it was better if he didn't so he could wash away the whole memory from his brain. He studied her face, and had to concede she was conventionally prettier than Marian, but Marian made love like she did everything: purposefully. Like it mattered.

The next morning, he was eating cereal when Will came downstairs. Both girls had disappeared.

"You didn't happen to see a pretty brunette run out of here, did you?"

"I would have remembered that."

"I don't know what happened to her roommate."

Nathan wasn't sure if Will knew more than he was letting on, but he just couldn't tell him the truth. Not about this. He might still find out through the women, but he had to risk offending him.

"Sounds like a good night."

"It was. I thought it might be an even better night, but hey it wasn't bad. You want to play some basketball later after class?"

"Sure. I'll meet you at the gym."

"Cool."

∽

Marian's mother begged her not to tell Nathan about her father's surgery. It was a "private family matter" and she needed to respect her father's wishes. In the end, she decided to shade the truth and tell him it was "elective surgery" so it wouldn't seem serious. Her mother insisted that they would get through *it* as a family—the "it" being cancer. They never spoke the word again, trying to convince themselves that lung cancer was not a death sentence. She pushed off Nathan's visit for a month, but she wasn't really sure her mother would allow it even then. She thought about visiting Nathan but she wanted to be at home in the event her parents needed her.

Unlike their first winter break apart, she decided that their relationship had progressed to a point where it could survive a little separation during the summer. She wrote him long letters about her days at home that never touched upon the anvil hanging over her family. She felt guilty omitting any discussion of her family crisis from her correspondence, but she had given her mother her word. Nathan wasn't much of a letter writer and she was content hearing his voice every night before she fell asleep. The string was broken one night after he had apparently fallen asleep reading. She had some worrisome thoughts, but chased them away. Nathan hadn't given her any reason to distrust him. She would be back at school soon and falling asleep on him again every night.

7

cigars

In the end, the unspoken word claimed Marian's father before the Fall semester began. Her mother wanted her to know that his "occasional" cigar was definitely *not* the cause according to his doctor. Honestly, Marian didn't know what her mother was trying to prove. Was it that he had no hand in his own demise or that she should mourn him as some sort of deity? Her mother was beyond ridiculous sometimes. Marian wanted to shake her to see if marbles would fall out of her ears, but that's not how she was raised. Instead, she let her mother think it mattered to her, if that's what helped her place it all in some warped perspective. Marian knew right then and there her mother would never marry again. After all, she had married the Great Man, and where could you go from there?

She wrote letters of apology to Nathan informing him of her father's passing maybe twenty times, but kept tearing them up. She knew it was cowardly, but she thought if she could only parse the right words it would make him understand how it was possible, she would withhold this information. But she just couldn't send it, no matter how eloquent it was. So, she dialed his number and waited, half hoping he wouldn't answer.

"Nathan?"

"Hey you. You sound weird."

"I feel weird."

"Everything okay?"

"No, I have something to tell you. My father is…..gone."

"Gone? He left your mother?"

"No. He is *gone*, gone. He died."

"From the elective surgery?"

"It wasn't really elective. I didn't tell you the whole truth and if you…"

"Wow. He died. From what?"

"Lung cancer."

"That seems quick."

"Who knows how long he had it. The surgery was probably too late."

"Why didn't you tell me?"

"I know you would have. My mother is so… well you know. Let's keep everything in the family. Stiff upper lip. All of that."

Nathan was trying to process that, while he was cheating on Marian, she was tending to her dying father. He felt like such a *dick*.

"It's okay. Don't worry about me."

"Thanks."

They spoke for a few more minutes and then Marian decided to end the conversation because it had gone better than expected. She wasn't really in the mood for small talk, anyhow. Nathan had switched at some point to a discussion of something that happened at his summer job at the school library and she couldn't concentrate.

∽

1962

Marian couldn't wait for her ninth birthday. She had inherited her mother's love of the outdoors and had promised her they could have a tea party in a nearby park. Marian had hoped to have her best friends there, but her father quickly squashed the idea. Her mother said her father wanted to have a "*more intimate family gathering*". She promised Marian she could have friends over, (secretly, she surmised), the day after her birthday for some cake. She knew her father would be at work. She didn't know exactly what her father's real objections were, but she knew enough to understand that he didn't really like having guests, and, when they did occasionally have people over, it usually didn't end well.

Marian's birthday fell on a Saturday which gave the Collingswood women time in the morning to pack the car with all the trappings of a faux royal tea party. Her father was stationed in his normal haunt on the porch smoking his repulsive cigars and reading the newspaper. Marian could see him peering skeptically atop his paper every once in a while. He was dressed in his weekend wear, meaning he looked like he could have been ready to head out to work. The only difference from his weekday dress was the absence of a tie. He used to tell Marian that no one expected to see a six-foot four man dressed in a tee shirt and jeans unless they were a bum or a farmer. She didn't exactly know what that meant, but she accepted his explanation and understood that he wasn't going to be playing hide and seek in their backyard like many of her friends' fathers. As education was important to him so he did read to her at night. There was that.

Her mother signaled to her father that the car was packed and he nodded in her direction. He came down off the porch and made sure they had packed at least two large blankets so as not to soil his clothes.

One of the few times that he consistently smiled was when he squeezed behind the wheel of his beloved Cadillac. Today was no different. He carefully placed his hands on the steering wheel, palms first, then fingers. He looked exceedingly pleased. Marian was old enough to know it wasn't practical, but, if she could have wished for anything, it would have been that they all could have lived in the Cadillac. For reasons she never fully grasped, her father seemed happiest behind the wheel of that car. While he drove to the park, he talked more than normal and even recited jokes (he was by no means a natural comedian) that made her mother smile. Marian knew he thought the whole thing was silly but at least he was playing along.

When they got to the park, her father immediately sought out a bench to light up a cigar while her mother spread out the blankets and other party paraphernalia. Marian was going to be the princess and her parents were playing the king and queen. She wore a tiara and her mother sported a crown. They knew better than to bring anything for her father to don. They had made finger cucumber sandwiches and wore frilly dresses and gloves. Marian found the concept of finger sandwiches very funny. She always imagined nibbling her own fingers. Her mother had made steeped tea and brought it, still piping hot, it in a thermos. When it was time for the tea to be served, they urged her father to come over and join the party. He begrudgingly agreed and stubbed out his cigar by crushing the tip against the bench which left an ash mark.

"Okay you sit here." Marian directed her mother to a folding chair at the head of the blanket.

"And you sit next to her." Marian directed her father to the folding chair next to her mother's.

"The King and Queen on their thrones." Marian beamed and her father had no choice but to comply. He sat up stick straight.

"Today we have a royal visitor from a faraway land," Marian announced.

"That's exciting news" Her mother chimed.

"Yes mother, our guests have traveled all the way from China."

Marian went to a pile and pulled out her prized china doll that her father brought back for her from his business trip to San Francisco the previous year. Her mother looked over at her father to see his reaction. He didn't say anything and her mother leaned over towards him and whispered: "She loves that doll. For a lot of reasons." Her father nodded in silence and forced a smile.

"Be careful with it honey." Her father warned. "Not inexpensive."

"Yes, Daddy."

"Has she brought us any gifts?" Her mother wanted to change the subject.

"Well, yes, she has." Marian went to her pile and came out

with costume jewelry and handed it to her mother as if they were precious.

"Expensive jewels from her homeland." Marian unclasped the necklace and placed it carefully around her mother's neck. For a second, Marian didn't think it would fit.

'Thank you. What's the princesses' name?"

"That's Princess Min."

"I like that name."

"I suppose I'm next?" Her father asked without emotion.

"Yes." Marian went back and pulled out a ratty red tie from her pile an brought it over. Her father didn't look happy. Her mother leaned over and whispered: "I had her take an old one." Marian handed it to her father and waited for his reaction.

"What would you like me to do with it honey?"

"Put it on. It's a valuable gift from the Princess."

Her father looked at her mother who made a face that indicated he would be in trouble if he refused their daughter. Her father rolled his eyes, but dutifully tied it as well as he could without a mirror. Marian held up the doll and then placed its face next to her ear.

"She said it's an honor to meet the King and Queen of Michigan."

"The honor is ours." Her mother replied and reflexively placed her hand on her husband's hand which was gripping the lawn chair arm. When she realized what her hand was resting on her mother quickly removed it. Marian looked at her and she saw that her clever daughter had accomplished what she had set out to do: she had her parents, who barely spoke or touched, sitting side by side nearly holding hands. Their eyes met and Marian broke into a wide smile. It was the perfect birthday gift.

She walked outside and found her mother on the porch blowing her nose. She waited until her mother composed herself before making her presence known. Her mother turned and crumpled up the tissue in her hands.

"My allergies are acting up again."

"It happens this time of year."

"How is Nathan?"

"Fine."

"You miss him?"

Marian was surprised by such a personal question from her.

"I do, actually."

"He seems like a nice boy."

"I don't think he's a boy, mother."

"You know what I mean. Everyone under thirty is a boy to me."

"Well, I'm glad you like him."

"So, you're serious about him."

"Yes. I love him."

"I can tell." Her mother smiled.

"It's obvious?"

"He loves you too?"

"I think so."

"He hasn't told you?"

Marian had never had a conversation with her mother about an impractical subject like love. She wasn't sure if there was a trap door she was about to fall through.

"He has, actually."

"That's good."

"When did Daddy tell you he loved you for the first time?"

Her mother didn't answer immediately, and Marian realized the answer. She decided to rescue her mother.

"Well, I know it was a long time ago. I almost forgot to tell you that Mrs. Harris came by to say how sorry she was and, not to worry, she would run the bake sale without you next Sunday."

"That woman is insufferable. I don't know how I ever involved myself with her."

"She always seems sort of nice."

"She has you fooled too."

"Anyhow, you have more important things to take care of than worrying about blueberry pies."

"I wanted to."

"Wanted to?"

"I wanted to say it too, but he never did."

"Oh. Daddy?"

"But I decided the words weren't as important as what he did. He was a good husband. And father."

"Yes," was all Marian could muster since she wasn't as forgiving as her mother. She seemed smaller than ever sitting there with her compromises and her rationalizations. Marian resolved that she would never bargain away her dignity for a man, no matter how desperate she was.

8

ties

The closet was finally empty, except for the rack of Nathan's ancient ties bolted to the back of the door. Her father always looked like he was born wearing a tie. Nathan, on the other hand, struggled to conform to the ritual of wearing one in the workplace. She was about to throw them all in a junk bag when the purple one caught her eye. She had been so proud of herself when she picked it out in a little shop in Como, Italy during their summer backpacking through Europe after college ended. She couldn't really picture Nathan in a tie every day, but someday it was bound to happen. She picked it up and playfully tied it around her neck, examining the exquisitely woven silk pattern of black and purple stripes. She remembered how Nathan had done the same thing in that cafe in Como. He draped the tie around his neck and let it hang down his stained tee shirt. She remembered the shirt because it bore the face of Jim Morrison, an image he sported almost as frequently as that of Jimi Hendrix. They had been dating for close to two years at that point. Her vision of their life together seemed so clear that she had stopped allowing for the possibility of any other outcome.

1973

They were almost out of money, so Nathan suggested that they sleep on the beach in Mykonos. She agreed, even though the sand was bound to be cold and she hated being cold almost as much as he hated being hot. It was the middle of August and they had been traveling for about ten weeks. Nathan seemed distracted as they approached the end of their adventure, but she didn't press him. Perhaps he was wondering what the end of college portended for them or maybe he was just as tired as she was of the lumpy mattresses, infrequent meals, and clothes that were usually washed once a week in a sink somewhere. She laughed to herself because out of everything, she knew the dirty clothes probably didn't matter to him. He seemed to ignore food falling on his shirts, like it was happening to someone else. She refrained from tidying him up even though she was dying to mother him.

She slept with as much of her body on him as he would allow to avoid touching the sand. As usual, he barely moved during the night but it still took her a long time to fall asleep. She ran her fingers over his patchy beard and wondered why some men always had gaps in their facial hair. Marian thought maybe it was the universe's way of telling some men they weren't supposed to grow beards. She was a little surprised Nathan didn't try to make love to her tonight since he always seemed to want to try out new places. She figured it wouldn't have been comfortable on the beach, but she was game if he really wanted to.

She worried sometimes that he would think that she might turn into her mother, so she pushed herself to be the girlfriend she thought he wanted her to be without shedding her identity.

She had avoided talking about what was next for them as long as she could stand it but she wasn't sure how much longer she could wait. Hoping he would bring it up, hadn't worked yet. She lived in Michigan and his family was in Maryland. She was willing to go just about anywhere to be with him, but she needed to hear that she had been drawn into the canvas as a permanent figure.

In the middle of the night her weight must have awakened him. He stirred and she fell on to the sand and woke up.

"Where are we?" He asked.

"The beach. In Mykonos."

"Oh yeah. Look at that." He pointed to the sky. There so many stars Marian thought that it could have been a Seurat painting.

"So, what happens in September?" Marian blurted out.

"September."

"The future."

"I've been thinking about that."

"You have?"

"Sure."

"Me too."

"I know. You're always thinking. Your whole face thinks with you." Nathan laughed.

"Genetic, I guess."

"To be honest, I hadn't given it much thought until you bought me that tie in Italy. That sort of freaked me out."

"It did?"

"It's purple, I wouldn't describe it as mature. Purple doesn't scream office job. Do you see yourself as mature?"

"Do you?"

Marian wasn't sure what the right answer was. Why was he asking her? Was she supposed to be honest? She selected the noncommittal middle ground.

"Sometimes."

"That's about right. I guess you know me too."

"So what have you been thinking?"

"I need to tell you something."

"That doesn't sound good."

"Remember the summer we were apart?"

What an idiot, how could she forget that summer.

"Kind of hard to forget."

"One night—"

"Are you *really* going to tell me this *now*?"

"I'm a coward."

"I don't need to know. It was just one night?"

"Yes. I—"

"That's all I need to know."

"You sure?"

"I'm sure. Do I have to worry about this happening again?"

"No. No, of course not. We're *us* now."

"So where are we living in September?"

"Wherever you want. I was thinking of New York."

Marian didn't want to reply right away and give him the

satisfaction of a quick affirmative response. Not after what he had just said. So, she waited and then finally spoke.

"I like that. Columbia has a writer's program I'm interested in."

Nathan wasn't sure they had really put his indiscretion behind them, but he wasn't about to push the issue tonight on a damp beach in Mykonos. She told him that the beach was too cold for her and that she was going to find a bench. He dutifully followed her to a bench overlooking the beach. He sat up and allowed her to put her head on his lap. He wasn't going to get much sleep tonight but the doghouse was better than no house.

9

sixty-five

Sixty-five. Nathan loved birthdays and probably would have made an elaborate gesture of some kind. It really didn't mean anything to her, except driving home the painful fact that she expected to be with Nathan today. Luckily, her daughter Mira would be coming over, which would distract her. She was hoping she might convince her to go the cemetery.

Marian had purchased some fresh flowers, and was arranging them on the kitchen table when she heard a knock. When she opened the door Mira was standing there with a long rectangular box.

"What in the world?"

"Mother. Move away from the door. This box is heavy."

Marian backed up and couldn't imagine what it was. Mira dragged the box inside to her living room and gently laid it on the floor. She began opening it.

"You're opening it?"
"Yes, before you try to stop me."
"What is it?"
"A high definition television."
"A television? Honey, you know I don't watch television. That was your father's thing."
"I know. I know. But you have no idea how many interesting programs are on now. It's a good companion, too."
"Ah, a companion. I don't need one."
"Just give it a chance, mother. If you don't like it in a few weeks, I'll bring it back."
Mira took a napkin off the kitchen table and wiped her forehead. Marian could see that Mira had gone to a lot of trouble, so she didn't want to reject her right away. She didn't have the luxury of a slate of loved ones knocking on her door every day. One daughter, her editor, a few cousins in Michigan, and some college friends scattered about the country was it. Not a very impressive list. Marian decided to show as much enthusiasm as she could muster up.
"It's quite a birthday present. Something your father might have dropped on me."
"Thank you. I'll take that as a compliment, however backhanded it might be."
"You're welcome. Much better response. I really think you'll enjoy it if you give it chance."
"I'm sure I will."
"So what are we going to do today after I set this up for you? Dinner at Luca's?"
"That would be nice. But can we go see your father first? I know it's not your first choice, but it would make me happy."

44 THE WIDOW *Verses*

Mira groaned but she knew she had been played beautifully. Her mother accepts the gift she doesn't really want, and may not keep. Then she has to go to the cemetery to "see" her father. Mira didn't get what purpose was served by placing him in the ground in front of a slab of stone. Why had her father not been cremated? The customs were so archaic and maudlin. She was astonished on one level that her *uber* pragmatic mother had any interest in the whole ritual. In the end, her mother the poet seemed to have carried the day when it came down to dealing with death.

"Nicely played, Marian. Yes, I'll go."

"Perfect. Let's have some tea first. Some nice green tea?"

"Sure."

Mira looked around as her mother put a kettle on the stove. There were some boxes in the corner of the living room that caught her eye.

"Mother?" Mira said out loud.

"What honey?"

"What are all these boxes?"

"Oh, I finally cleared out your father's closet."

"Good for you. Given all the crap he kept, that probably took a good week."

Marian came over and set down a Minnie Mouse mug with a tea bag in front of Mira.

"Seriously? My Minnie Mouse mug? From like a hundred years ago?"

"Just a habit, I guess."

"I *am* 32, right?"

"I guess your father rubbed off on me."

"So did you find anything interesting in there?"

"A few things."

"Did he have some old Cardinals crap from like the 1930s? Dizzy Dean's smelly socks or something?" Mira laughed.

"Nothing like that. A few caps and some old balls. You can take whatever you want."

"I don't know."

"It might be nice to have something."

"I'll take a look after I finish my tea."

Mira looked through the junk boxes first for some reason. She thought maybe her mother would consider some important piece of her childhood as disposable. But it really was just junk like her father's old ties, wallets, brushes, and other assorted rubbish. The boxes labeled *Mementos* were much more interesting. It was like taking a walk back through her childhood. The baseball games. Five Hundred Rummy with his Golden Nugget cards. Listening to Santana and Crosby, Stills & Nash on his old LPs that looked like they were more junk than treasure. She heard *Dark Star* playing in her brain and it made her smile. Her father sang along to all of his music, but he couldn't really carry a tune. She knew he thought he had a pleasant voice and no one had the heart to tell him otherwise.

"I think I want some of the records."

"Then they're yours. What are you going to do with them?"

"I don't know. Maybe I'll get a turntable."

"Your father would be happy. So why don't we go now? Did you finish your tea?"

"I'm done."

The drive to the cemetery took about twenty minutes. On the way Mira thought about telling her mother she was thinking of moving with her boyfriend to Seattle, but she just couldn't find the right words. Instead, they discussed her mother's latest work.

"So my agent called the other day and said he might need to find me a new publisher."

"Why?"

"It appears my publisher is about to be swallowed up and the new company has no interest in poetry."

"That's silly."

"When was the last time you discussed poetry with your friends?"

"Other than complaining about my mother, the poet?"

"I always told your father you should have been a comedy writer."

"And what did he say back?"

"That he was glad you got his sense of humor."

"He was right about that. So, you still laboring over that new work?"

"Sometimes. Comes and goes. Anyhow, now I have no deadline. Apparently, they will release me from any current contract I have."

"Wow. Free money to write. I like that."

"I just hope he finds a new publisher. I don't have the patience at my age to publish it myself."

"People love your poetry. I think someone will publish you, mother."

"Old news is old news. Stop in front of the main building here. Keep the car running. I'll be back in a minute."

Marian went inside and Mira looked around. There was a hearse off in the distance with mourners huddled around a gravesite. Why did she let her mother drag her here? She felt a rain drop on her nose and looked up. Some dark gray clouds had moved overhead. A few minutes later her mother reappeared.

"What was that about?"
"Just some gardening suggestions."
"Really?"
"Leave me alone. You know me. Let's go."
Marian directed Mira to Nathan's grave. To her surprise, there was a man standing near the grave looking at the inscription. Marian immediately saw it was the man with the movie star gray hair.
"Can I help you?" Marian asked almost too brightly.
"Hello. I was just admiring the words."

> *I am the air you breathe*
> *and you are*
> *the star I follow*
> *I am the anchor*
> *you hold fast to*
> *and you are*
> *the moon that lights*
> *every dark corner*
> *I am the shelter*
> *that provides you sanctuary*
> *and you are*
> *the beginning and*
> *I am the end*

"Who is the poet?"
"It's from one of my mother's poems. She's a *prominent* poet." Mira felt the need to set the record straight, especially after her mother just lost her publisher.
"Forgive my ignorance. It's beautiful."

"Thank you. That's very kind of you." Marian tried to change the tone of the conversation. She was a little surprised Mira felt the need to dress him down.

"What is your name?"

"Marian. Collingswood."

"Nice to meet you Marian Collingswood . I'm Charles Norman. Sorry to have disturbed your visit."

"Not at all. I'm sorry for your loss."

"Thank you. I'll be on my way." He nodded goodbye to Mira and she nodded back. Marian watched him walk back towards his wife's grave.

"You think he's handsome, don't you?" Mira came over and whispered in her mother's ear.

"What are you talking about? Hand me those flowers."

Mira gave her mother the flowers and didn't press the issue for now. Marian kneeled down and started planting the fresh flowers. She looked up and glanced over at Charles as he walked away. He liked her poetry so there was that.

10

company

1974

The fifteen-foot ceilings and elegant painted-over crown moldings were a tease. Every time Marian looked up she saw the bygone grandeur that some very wealthy couple enjoyed decades ago. She and Nathan were living in a tiny sliver of what was a four-story house on the upper west side. The bedroom was just that, a room with a bed and no space for even a speck of furniture. They had some milk crates that doubled as end tables and storage units. It had the typical Manhattan kitchen which consisted of a stove top and an aging refrigerator that looked like something her grandfather referred to as an *icebox*, when she was a child. She had envisioned cooking meals for Nathan when the spirit moved her, but it was such a chore, she rarely did. The whole apartment would heat up and everything would absorb the smell of the food.

For some reason she had invited her classmate Ellen and her boyfriend over for dinner. She had never been very impressed with Ellen's work and wondered when one of the professors was going to advise her that she needed to find another vocation. Perhaps she could write news articles. Marian could tell by their uninterested expressions that her classmates also found her stories tedious. She was, however, such a kind soul that Marian enjoyed her company, hoping that their association would make her a better person somehow.

Nathan was always open to meeting new acquaintances, so he didn't protest when she told him they were having company on Friday night. When she told him Ellen's boyfriend was a stockbroker he blanched, but said he hoped he was a sports fan. Nathan had found his way into advertising, which didn't satisfy him. However, he rationalized that at least it was about selling products people needed, for the most part. Unlike the stock market, which seemed to be glorified gambling as far as he could tell.

Marian was cutting up fruit when the bell rang. Nathan opened the door and was surprised to see an attractive, waif like girl standing next to a man at least a foot taller than her. Nathan was just under six feet and felt like his hand was swallowed up by Todd, who introduced himself. It wasn't long before he found out he had played offensive line for Syracuse. Some booster had greased the wheels for him and he actually didn't know much about stocks. He was trying to learn.

"Did you see the Thrilla in Manila?" Todd asked. "What a fight!"

Nathan could see that Todd was even more enthusiastic about sports than he was. Maybe this night wouldn't be a chore.

"I was rooting for Frazier. There's something about Ali."

"Oh, I hear you. Bit of a braggadocio," Todd agreed.

"Just a bit."

"Manila?" Marian exclaimed from the kitchen area.

"Boxing, honey." Nathan informed her.

"Brutal," Ellen chimed in.

"It can be Ellen. Not my favorite sport, but there's something compelling about some of the bigger fights."

"What's your favorite sport, Nathan?" Ellen inquired.

"Please don't get him started on baseball, Ellen." Marian pleaded as she put down a tray of fruit and some cheese and crackers.

"My father used to take me to Cubs' games." Ellen said.

"Now you've gone and done it." Marian said in mock horror.

"The Cubs, Ellen? And I was just starting to like you and your wise old man." Nathan smiled, so she would know he was half joking.

"Ah, a Cards fan."

"Diehard."

"I watch the World Series," Todd offered. "But that's about it."

"Okay, I think we can move on from the sports portion of our evening," Marian gently offered. Nathan took the hint.

"So what kind of book are you writing for your thesis Ellen? Are you a poet too?" Nathan asked. Marian gave him a look that he didn't quite understand. He only knew his inquiry was some sort of misstep.

"It's a novel. I'm not much of a poet. I guess you would call it historical fiction."

"That sounds interesting."

"I'm still shaping it. Your girlfriend, on the other hand, is already causing quite the stir among the faculty."

"Ellen."

"Don't be bashful Marian. You know what I'm saying is true."

"A stir, huh?"

"There are some agents knocking down her door as well."

"Is that true?" Nathan asked her.

"A few of my professors have made some contacts. Nothing concrete." Marian tried to downplay Ellen's revelations.

Nathan could tell he wasn't getting the whole story from Marian but decided to let it go before they had a row in public. It was curious why she hadn't mentioned anything.

"Your woman is the *it* gal, Nathan. Buckle up for the ride."

"I'm buckled in, Ellen."

"I'm proud of her," Ellen said without a hint of jealousy.

"Thanks Ellen." Marian said.

In the end, Marian considered the evening a success. Nathan seemed to get on with Todd and she knew he had to like Ellen. Who didn't? As she washed the dishes she wondered if he would make a big fuss about what Ellen had said. She had deliberately avoided giving him any details about school in recent months. She didn't want him to feel somehow inferior, even though they were in different professions.

"So why didn't you tell me about all of the things going on at school?" Nathan asked from the living room.

"Oh, I still don't know where it's all going, so I didn't want to get my hopes up or yours for that matter."

She didn't turn around and continued to wash the dishes to avoid him seeing her face since he could read her so well. He came up behind her and put his arms around her waist and kissed her neck. She stopped washing the dishes and turned around. A few minutes later they were making love in their cramped bedroom. When they were relaxing, he asked, "Sort of an odd match. No?"

"He wasn't what I was expecting. I didn't imagine her with a football player."

"What was that look you gave me earlier when I asked about her writing?"

"She's a sweetheart as you can see, but not much of a writer."

"Oh. That's unfortunate."

"It is."

"So that's what it feels like."

"What feels like?"

"To make love to a famous poet."

"Hah."

"It was a little more exciting, I think."

"Okay. I got it."

"I wonder what it would it be like to be married to a famous poet?"

Marian turned around and Nathan was holding a diamond ring. Emerald cut. She sat up in bed and he held it out for her. He asked her to marry her that night and she got up three or four times to look at herself in the mirror and model the ring from different angles. She wasn't expecting to feel like a giddy school girl, but the ring seemed to exert more power over her than she was expecting. The last time she got out of bed she walked over to the window by the street. In another era she could imagine the owners of this brownstone coming home by horse drawn carriage. The chivalrous husband helping his wife down and then up the stairs. How did he propose to her? On a Central Park carriage ride? They probably slept like royalty in one of the larger apartments upstairs in a grand canopy bed. Nathan's snoring broke the spell and she watched a cat jump on top of a parked car before disappearing. She walked back to the bedroom and looked at her ring one last time before lying down. Nathan rolled over and smiled in his sleep. He wasn't a prince, but tonight, she felt a little like a princess.

11

stickball

Marian could never understand why anyone would possibly need hundreds of television channels. Or how anyone could ever find anything they actually wanted to watch. It seemed like a superhighway with hundreds of off-ramps and no signs. She figured she must have wasted twenty minutes of valuable time clicking through channels before she decided to turn it off. The remote control was also daunting with buttons that had different shapes, sizes, and colors. She must have pressed every button twice before she found the power button. Marian didn't like lying, so now at-least she could truthfully tell Mira she had "watched" television. A few minutes, after she put the remote down, her agent called with news.

"Marian?"

"Andrew."

"I have some news. The new publisher wants to see a draft of your latest book."

"They do? I thought my work was too esoteric."
"Nobody said that."
"So why would I want to be in bed with these people?"
"Because legally they still own you."
"I never liked lawyers."
"So how far along are you?"
"Hard to say."
"Half? Two thirds?"
"You know it doesn't work like that."
"I know. I know. But I need to tell them something."
"Tell them half then. That should put them off for a while."
"I'll say sixty percent. Sounds better. Okay?"
"Alright. It sounds ridiculous, but you know how to play this game better than me."

Marian said goodbye and sat down in what Nathan called her "thinking chair". It was the most uncomfortable chair in the house, which focused the mind. Marian had begun to cozy up to the idea that she wasn't under any pressure to write. Now, she needed to re-engage with the themes she had begun to explore. Of course, she couldn't tell Andrew that she had only completed one poem since Nathan's passing. The task ahead seemed daunting. She was starting to feel overwhelmed and decided to pour herself a glass of wine, which lead to three, before she started having nightmares with scary stranger's knocking on her door to repossess her furniture and take her away to debtor's prison.

∽

Nathan could feel the bones in her back, which was a new sensation. He had called Ellen to make sure someone was giving

Marian a bachelorette party. Marian wasn't really the bachelorette party type, but he told himself perhaps she should have one anyhow. After all, he intended to have a party with his friends and he didn't really want to feel guilty. He thought Ellen might think it odd that he was calling her, but she was surprisingly chatty when he called, as if they had an intimate relationship. They agreed to meet for a drink in a bar close to her apartment on 99th street off of Broadway. Her neighborhood was in that no man's land between the upper west side and Morningside Heights that was mostly dominated by some projects, bodegas, and fast food joints.

The bar was apiece with the neighborhood and he was surprised that she seemed so comfortable there. The bartender even seemed to know her and he smiled at Nathan, which was unsettling for some reason. Coming from suburban Maryland, he never quite understood how parochial Manhattan was. Amid the density and chaos, every few blocks encompassed a small neighborhood where people seemed to be at least familiar with each other. Before he knew it they each had downed three or four drinks and he wasn't even sure they had discussed the bachelorette party. Marian had told him that she was some sort of saintly character, but clearly Marian had not spent enough time with her to appreciate the full picture. This girl liked her alcohol. Nathan was no lightweight, but since school had ended, he didn't have the same stamina. With his decision making already impaired from all the alcohol, he agreed to go to her apartment when she told him she had some really good weed back there.

It was really good weed, but there was a moment when Nathan looked at the door of her apartment and knew he should have left. None of the reasons running in his head persuaded him, and a few minutes later she was moving closer to him on the couch. It was a funny thing about kissing someone when you were drunk, Nathan thought. It always felt like you had never kissed anyone before that moment. Years later, when his memories lead him back to that afternoon, it was the kiss that he would remember.

After they were finished Ellen got off the couch and pulled on her underwear. He waited for her to express some regret about what they had just did, but all she asked was what he wanted in his coffee. They drank their coffee in silence and then Nathan pulled on his clothes and told her he needed to go. He walked home so he could sober up more and tried to figure out why he had slept with Ellen. And, why she had slept with him. Was there something wrong with him? Was he scared of marriage? A little Puerto Rican boy was playing stickball in the street and he hit the pink ball right at Nathan who caught it. He held the ball for a few seconds before threw it back. He wished he could ask to join them.

12

tea

For a week, Marian used all her old tricks. Quiet tea in the garden. Walks in her favorite park. Hours in the chair with no padding. But nothing of consequence was created. She knew what this book was going to be about, grief. What else walked next to her, day in and day out but her constant companion grief? The problem was that she couldn't step back and see it. It was too close. So, her poems were all emotion without any insight and, therefore, of no use to anyone.

There was a tea shop that had opened up last winter on the street that ran past the barber shop where Nathan got his hair cut. Mira used to go with him and she would drop them off sometimes. When she arrived early to pick them up, she would see Mira standing next to him with a lollipop and he would be chatting away with the barber. Sometimes she just stood outside the window and watched their interactions. One of her favorite poems was written on one of those days.

I am a tree
standing guard
Or maybe just a leaf
floating by
a barber's window
but I can see in
and they
cannot see me as
my daughter worships
her father
unaware he is a deity
sitting in a leather chair
instead of a throne
with his hair
flying about
His laughter
making her smile
so I can see
her lollipop
turning her tongue
a lovely shade of green
to match the color of the leaf
I have become
in my secret world

Marian walked in and looked around. There were only about five tables but since it was the early morning there weren't any students camped out with laptops. She decided to take a seat in the back of the shop, facing the wall and sat down. A young man took her order and convinced her to try some new Indian tea when she hesitated. She also ordered a chocolate covered biscuit that had been staring at her from its perch on the counter as she walked by. The tea had a cinnamon flavor with a hint of some other aromatic spices she couldn't place. She took out her notebook and pen and sat back and sipped her tea. She looked down to dip her biscuit in the tea when she heard a vaguely familiar voice.

"Hello, Marian."

To her surprise, she looked up to see Charles from the cemetery. It bothered her that she couldn't remember his last name.

"Charles. Nice to see you."

"Flattered that you remembered."

"I don't speak to many people at the cemetery." Marian smiled.

"So, I see you found one of my favorite new places in town."

"I like it in the morning. It gets *young* in the afternoon."

"Agreed. I see you have paper and pen. I don't want to interrupt you."

"No, not at all. Not much happening there. Have a seat."

Marian noted how well-dressed he was. His sport coat was made of fine wool and his shirt, which had French cuffs, looked like it came from an upscale shop.

"Thank you."

"So, I presume you live in town?"

"I do. Forty years now. You?"

"Not much less than that."

"Do you mind if I ask you about your writing?"

"Not at all. I have been writing poetry since I can remember. I've published ten volumes. Supposed to be eleven but it's coming along slowly."

"I bought your first book. I'm enjoying it, though I have to admit it's challenging. I'm not used to reading poetry. I'm an avid reader of fiction."

"You bought *Underground*? That's very flattering. Good to know it's in print somewhere." She laughed.

"Oh, you have many in print."

The waiter came over and Charles ordered the same tea that Marian was sipping.

"So enough about me. What do you do for work?"

"Did. Semi-retired now. I had an importing business. I turned it over to my oldest son."

"What did you import?"

"Mostly French goods. Wine. Some other less exciting items."

"So, you must have made many trips to France?"

"Many. I purposely sought out a business that would allow me to travel to Europe. I knew when I went to Paris as a young man, I wanted to connect to that city somehow. I am an unabashed Francophile. No getting around it."

"I presume you speak French?"

" je suis heureux de vous avoir rencontré"

"Sounds wonderful."

"I am pleased to have met you, roughly translated."

"See I knew it was something nice."

"Have you been to France?"

"I have. My husband Nathan and I went a few times alone, and we took my daughter, Mira, there when she was maybe twelve."

"I like that name. Mira."

"So did Nathan. He let me pick."

"How long has he been gone?"

"Over a year now. I know your loss is more recent. I'm so sorry."

"Thank you. Nathalie was her name. She was French actually. We met in Paris on one of my trips. My first trip. I lured her here. Though I have to admit, I don't think she ever really got over leaving France, which is understandable."

"I give her a lot of credit. That couldn't have been easy."

"We stayed connected to her family, but you're right, it's not the same."

"So what brings you into town?"

"Just poking around. I didn't feel like going into the office today. I have that luxury these days."

"I like that. Poking around. You don't hear that expression much anymore."

"Feel free to use it in one of your poems."

He had a nice smile. She was always a sucker for a nice smile.

"I may just do that."

"So, is Mira your only child?"

"She is. We talked about having a second but, in the end, I think we liked the freedom. Once Mira got to be about five or six it seemed like we had the best of both worlds. Does that sound selfish?"

"No. Just a life choice. It sounds pretty logical. I think Nathalie wanted a large family given that she wasn't in her own country but two seemed like a big enough challenge to me."

"So, you have how many?"

"Two. A daughter and a son."

"Nice."

"Well, I don't want to overstay my welcome. You didn't come here to talk with me. Hopefully, I'll see you around town again."

"Going back to poking around?"

"Going to see what sort of trouble I can stir up."

He subtly nodded to her in a perceptibly chivalrous gesture and left the tea shop. Funny thing was he forgot to pay for his tea. Marian figured she could hold that over his head the next time she saw him. Then, she caught herself. They might never see each other again. Maybe Mira was right. She had enjoyed his company and there was no getting around that he was a handsome man. She took out a compact and looked at herself. Not exactly a blushing bride staring back at her. Her hair was falling down below her ears and threatening to take off in new directions. Not a stitch of makeup. Not that she ever really wore much. She surmised he was probably just lonely and she happened to be there. She looked down at her blank pad and wrote the words: *poking around*.

13

nathalie

1978

She had said to hug the right bank north to their office. It sounded innocuous enough. What she didn't say was that he might never make it to their office because the right bank was teeming with artists, booksellers, and other denizens of the river that were too fascinating to ignore. How could anyone possibly get any work accomplished in this city? As far as Charles could see, it was like strolling through a postcard without any discernible end point. He had already spent too much time at Notre Dame taking pictures and he was going to be late. He took one last look back at the church. He loved how it guarded the river looking like a two-towered stone sentinel.

The office was a few blocks from the Seine on a typically

charming side street. He peered into a patisserie window to make sure his tie was straight and his hair looked presentable. A woman who looked far too old to be on her feet all day was watching him from behind the counter and smiled at him. He acknowledged her and thought back to his conversations with Isabelle, the agent. He never tired of hearing her answer the phone with that bewitching accent. She sounded about thirty and she had promised him a tour of the city. In his mind, she was a blend of the girl next door—not very intimidating, maybe attainable—and Brigitte Bardot—terrifying, unattainable. Her company represented some of the best vineyards in Bordeaux and he knew they were very selective about who they would allow to import and sell their wine. Charles had done his homework and he knew they had no distributor in the Eastern part of the country, so it was an opportunity of a lifetime.

The office was on the second floor, and when he pushed the old wooden door open, an exquisite young woman was sitting behind a desk in the reception area. When he tried some of his French, she smiled and to his relief said she spoke English.

"Are you Isabelle?"

She laughed, which confused him.

"Ms. Angelle is the owner. I can get her for you."

"Is that Isabelle?"

"Oui. Yes."

"What's your name?"

"Nathalie. Are you the American from New York she was expecting?"

"I hope so."

"I think you are quite a bit... younger than she was expecting."

"Oh."

"I'm sure it will be fine. Let me go and tell her you are here."
Nathalie began to walk away and then turned quickly back to Charles.

"And I would stay with English. Your French is not so good. Like my English."

"Better than my French. Thanks."

Nathalie walked away again and this time she disappeared behind closed doors. Charles could see that she had left some books open on her desk. From the photos, it looked like she was reading art history. A few moments later, a tiny woman with horn-rimmed glasses who appeared to be in her fifties and possessed an imperious manner shook his hand. Charles had to recalculate quickly.

"Thank you for meeting with me."

"Nathalie tells me you are alone?"

"Yes."

"You have no business partners?"

"No. Just employees."

"I see."

"I was expecting—"

"Someone older."

"Frankly, yes. The vineyards we represent are institutions with impeccable reputations."

"I understand."

"So we must be able to trust that their wines are in the most experienced hands."

"I would not have come to Paris or bothered you unless I was passionate about this. I have dedicated my life to wine."

"Your life? Is your family in the wine business?"

"No. They aren't. I have no history to provide you. But I can show you what I've accomplished so far with my business."

Charles self-consciously patted his briefcase containing his papers. Isabelle looked over at Nathalie who was listening. She could see that Nathalie had taken a shine to this American. She was normally buried in her art books and had little interest in the affairs of the office.

"Come back to my office and show me what you've brought." As soon as Isabelle shut her office door she spoke.

"I didn't want to embarrass you, but the people I represent would never accept you. I'm sorry you came all this way."

"Oh. Are you sure? Can I show what I've brought? Five minutes of your time, s'il vous plaît?"

Charles looked at her the way her fourteen-year-old did when she told him something he didn't want to hear. She had yelled at him this morning to pick up his clothes off the floor and all she got was a shrug. She had wanted to smack him, but she held back for fear of sending their relationship spiraling to a new low.

"Five minutes."

∽

Charles felt as if he was in a Godard film. There was nothing particularly remarkable about the brasserie, but it was so French. He tried to contain his excitement so Nathalie didn't think he was some unsophisticated American. He really wanted to shake the hand of the waiter, but he knew how silly that would look. In the natural light, she was even prettier than he thought. He was wondering if she agreed to have a drink with him because she surmised, he might have traveled all the way to Paris for a five-minute meeting.

"She seems pretty tough."
"Tough?"
"Difficult?"
"Ah. Yes, sometimes. She is not the happiest of people."
"I don't think she liked me very much."
"She is not easy to…decipher?"
"I understand. I know I'm not what she expected."
"No. That's true. So, what do you think of Paris?"
"Magnifique."
Nathalie laughed, but he wasn't sure if she was laughing at his poor pronunciation.
"Are you an art student?"
"You must be a detective."
"I can read upside down."
"Ah. My books. Yes, I am trying."
"Do you paint?"
"Oui. I mean, yes."
"What do you paint?"
"Whatever I find interesting. Like you."
"You're going to paint me?"
"Maybe someday."

She smiled and Charles envisioned himself lying on a couch in the nude like a Rubens' figure. He tried not to laugh out loud at the ridiculous image that popped into his head.

"Maybe you'll be famous someday, and I'll have a story to tell my grandchildren."

"And how would that story begin and end?"

Charles took a long sip of his beer to consider his response. She seemed to be studying him. He wondered, he hoped, her question was something more than an off-hand inquiry.

"Maybe after another beer I'll have more clarity." Charles gave what he hoped was a half-smile.

"So, that's the master plan."

"No. No plan. If I had a good plan I might have been more successful today with Isabelle."

"I think she actually liked you. If she didn't then you would never have made it to her office. Many have never made it past my desk."

"I guess that's something."

"And none have ever made it to where you are."

"So maybe I will have a story."

"Maybe."

Nathalie had a mischievous grin on her face, and Charles sat back, trying to take it all in. There were dirty blonde curls falling into and framing her face and he was dying to push one of them to the side and kiss her. He had a feeling she was reading his mind. He might never leave France.

14

launch

1975

Marian's professor's apartment on West End Avenue may have been a few blocks away, but it may as well have been miles away. Such was life in New York City. The doorman greeted them as they stepped inside the building and directed them to his apartment. To her surprise, the dimly lit hallways and carpet were a bit dated, making you unprepared for the opulence of the interior of his apartment. A young woman who was working in the kitchen opened the door and ushered them into the living room. There looked to be at-least three bedrooms ringing a great room. There was a long wall of cherry wood shelves teeming with books. The room seemed to stretch so far from the door that Marian wasn't completely sure the man walking towards them was Professor Walters until he passed the kitchen area.

"Marian. And you must be Nathan. Let me have your coats."

"Thank you."

Marian could see there were delicate dishes meticulously arranged in various stations throughout the apartment and a bar with wine and hard liquor. Nathan gave her a look that meant he was impressed. Professor Walters returned from one of the bedrooms.

"So, this is the man that has captured the heart of my star student?"

"That would be me." Nathan confirmed with a forced smile.

"Thank you for allowing me to share her these past two years."

"She's used to being passed around."

Marian playfully hit Nathan on the shoulder and he feigned injury.

"Well you should be very proud of her. The *Times* is going to review her first book. That doesn't happen every day."

"I am. This is quite the apartment."

"Oh thanks. I can't take credit for anything, except the books. Those are my children."

"Then you have lots of mouths to feed." Nathan grinned.

"Indeed."

"So, who's coming to the party?"

"I invited a lot of my contacts in the literary world, and some colleagues from the university."

"That's very kind of you." Nathan said.

"I believe in this young lady."

"Professor Walters steered me toward poetry after reading some of my work early in the program. I was ready to write novels."

"Is that right?" Nathan asked in a slightly bored tone.

"I may have nudged her in that direction. Wasn't hard to see the talent. I think it may have been a poem about you that piqued my interest."

"Me?"

"I'm sure you've read it."

"Not sure."

Nathan looked for some signal from Marian that he was in error, but he received no explanation and an awkward silence ensued. Professor Walters could see they needed their privacy. He asked them if they wanted drinks and left to pour them wine.

"What's he talking about?"

"It's just a poem about love. It's not about you specifically, so don't worry."

"I'm not worried. I like the cover you picked. I'm not sure if I told you that."

"No, you haven't. That's okay. I know you're busy. I didn't actually pick the cover. The publisher came up with most of it."

"Oh."

"Let's just enjoy the party."

Nathan leaned over and kissed her on the cheek. She shivered. His lips were still cold from the outside. The doorbell started ringing and Professor Walters handed them their glasses of red wine on his way to the door. As guests began to fill the apartment, Nathan stood back and watched as each of them was introduced to Marian by the Professor. He drank his wine quickly and decided he needed some more. He flagged down an attendant walking nearby and exchanged his empty glass for a full one. The guest list appeared to be mostly older men, but an attractive older woman in an expensive yellow dress was looking at the Professor's book collection. She looked vaguely familiar.

He gulped down the rest of his wine and decided to amuse himself. He looked to see where Marian was and couldn't find her.

"Hello."

She turned to him and smiled.

"Hello there. You are?"

"Nathan."

She stuck out her hand and he shook it. He could smell her perfume now.

"Do I know you?"

"I don't know. Where would we know each other from?"

"The neighborhood?"

"I do live nearby. You?"

"Same."

"What brings you here?"

"Um. My wife. It's her book party."

"Oh. Lucky man."

An attendant walked by and Nathan decided to refresh his wine glass again. He was starting to feel lighter.

"Do you know the Professor?"

"We have mutual friends. Been to a lot of the same parties. He thought I might enjoy this one."

"Are you?"

"Now I am."

She smiled and he tried to peg her age. Maybe 40. Well preserved. Out of the corner of his eye he could see that Marian had come into his field of view and was now watching him.

"What do you do? Besides marrying well."

She laughed and he forced a smile.

"Public relations. Advertising."

"Convincing the masses to buy what they don't need."

"Sometimes. Do you do anything? I mean, for…"

"I know what you mean. I keep busy. My husband is a publisher."

Nathan was trying not to focus on the part of her dress that had now opened so that he could see her breast tucked into a white bra. He could see that she was aware of his interest in the condition of her dress. She looked pleased.

"I think your wife is walking towards us. Perhaps I'll see you in the neighborhood."

Nathan couldn't think of something snappy to say so he just nodded his head in agreement just as Marian arrived.

"Your husband was just telling me how talented you are. Jocelyn Remsen."

Jocelyn put out her hand and Marian shook it.

"Is that right? He's my cheerleader. Can I grab him for a moment? There are some people I want him to meet."

"He's *all* yours. Nice to meet you. Good luck with the book."

"Thank you."

When they were out of earshot Marian leaned over and whispered.

"Are you drunk?"

"No. Maybe a little."

"Nathan. Don't embarrass me."

"Of course not."

"Who was that?"

"I don't know. Some publisher's wife."

"I'm cutting you off. No more drinks."

"Done."

She didn't know whether she could trust him. For the rest of the party she kept him close by and he didn't say anything stupid. However, she could tell he had no interest in the people he was introduced to. The last time he had smiled that night was when he was flirting with the woman in the yellow dress. She knew that he didn't really have something he was passionate about other than his beloved Cardinals and music. Was she ever going to be enough for him?

15

new orleans

When Nathan was alive, his snoring would awaken Marian and she would go downstairs to sleep on the daybed. Her bedroom was perfectly quiet now, and yet there were many occasions like this evening when she still couldn't sleep through the night. She would lay there and play with word combinations in her brain. Then, she would stop and review her unexpected meeting with Charles in the tea shop. He wasn't really her type. She had consciously avoided any man who might remind her of her own father and there was something about the way he carried himself that echoed her father's manner. When Mira called her tonight, she didn't share her chance meeting with Charles. She knew Mira would say something that would make her feel uncomfortable. Could she ever speak with her daughter about a man who was not her father? She understood there were lots of mothers who treated their daughters like their best friends and confidantes, but she needed boundaries.

Marian finally decided to get up and go downstairs to make some tea. She turned on the stove and sat down in front of her new television and clicked it on. She figured out how to change the channels and came upon a cooking show with an over-caffeinated man who was so excited about what he was creating. She wondered if chefs felt the same way she did when she finished writing a particularly satisfying sentence that didn't exist a few moments before her pen had touched the page. She didn't want to be shallow, but whatever dish that man was cooking would be gone as quickly as it was created. She hoped her words could be savored as long as books were printed and people still needed to explore the mystery of human experience.

1980

When Nathan suggested they go to New Orleans, Marian wasn't opposed to the idea, but she wondered if that kind of trip had passed her by. She was twenty-seven and her days of drinking to excess and stumbling down the street seemed like another lifetime. She was focused on her work now, and had found a rhythm in her daily routine that she was content to follow. New York wasn't the easiest place to live but, as the end of the 70's dawned, the messiness of the city gave her endless paths to explore. As she looked outside her airplane window ten thousand feet above the city she was struck by how orderly it looked. You would have no idea from up here just how chaotic New York was and how every street revealed something different.

When they arrived at their hotel Nathan seemed energized by the adventure. Their lovemaking had lapsed into a pattern that satisfied Marian, although she sensed that Nathan was going through the motions on some nights. Marian was about to open her suitcase to put her clothes in a drawer when she felt him grab her from behind. He pulled down her skirt and underwear and put his hand between her legs. She couldn't see his face, but she could hear his breathing. It became more labored as he started to thrust from behind. He usually waited for her to have an orgasm first but today he let himself go. When she finally turned around, he was already pulling his shorts up.

"Sorry, couldn't hold it."

"That's okay."

"Want to explore?"

"Sure."

On the elevator Marian searched for his hand. As her hand touched his she realized that it has been quite some time since they had actually held hands. Though they were forced to break their grip on each other when they walked through the narrow front door, Marian made a point of finding his hand again. The humidity coming off Lake Pontchartrain was oppressive. By the time they walked into the French quarter they both needed showers. Before they could make it into a restaurant the threatening clouds unburdened themselves of their moisture and they were drenched when they sat down.

"That was a fun walk," Marian said while trying to unstick her shirt from her body.

"But it was kind of cool right? You don't see that in New York."

"Not that sudden."

"So I have some news."

"Do I need a drink?"

Nathan knew exactly what she meant, but kept going.

"I quit my job."

"Quit?"

"I couldn't take it anymore."

"I had no idea you were that unhappy. Did something happen?"

"I couldn't work for Shelly anymore."

"I know you've told me he can be abusive but…"

"Abusive? The guy rides you and sucks the life out of you and then takes all the credit."

"I didn't realize. You couldn't wait?"

"Wait for what? To be stripped of the little dignity I have left? Fuck him. Fuck them."

A woman at a table heard Nathan use profanity and looked up from her conversation. Nathan gave her a mocking smile. The waitress came by and asked for their order. Nathan ordered Hurricanes for both of them, though Marian told him it was a little early to start drinking. He assured her that, if necessary, he would finish both drinks. Marian was now really concerned that this trip was going to be a disaster given his mood. Marian drank about half of her Hurricane which tasted too good to contain three kinds of liquor. Half the tall glass was enough to make her tipsy. True to his word, Nathan finished her drink and was clearly feeling the effects. The rain had stopped almost as suddenly as it began, and the water was streaming into the sewers. The sax and trombone players were back on the streets looking for tips as the strains of jazz music drifted in the air. Nathan put his arm around her shoulder and she put her hand in his back pocket as they walked aimlessly along Bourbon Street.

Marian wanted to continue the conversation about his job, but she could tell he wasn't in the mood to discuss it. There was no need to ruin their weekend getaway. She just wished that he could find some vocation that truly interested him. Her agent had let her know that she was going to go on a book tour soon and now she was worried about leaving him alone. It was only two weeks, but that seemed like a long time now that he had no job to occupy him while she was away.

"You have that look."

"What look?"

"The Marian is worrying about something look."

"No worries."

"I just told you I quit my job, and you have no worries?"

"Not really. Sometimes the burden of remaining in a job you despise is worse than not having a job at all."

"Ah."

"I just want you to be happy, that's all."

"The world will be alright with one less Adman."

"You can find another job."

"In advertising?"

"With your experience, sure."

"I don't know what I want to do, besides drinking another Hurricane."

"We'll figure it out."

They wandered the streets that afternoon and lounged in jazz bars while trying to forget about Nathan's troubles. He got progressively more inebriated, and by the time they made it back to the hotel that first night, he was barely able to walk. Marian pushed him into bed with his clothes on and took his sandals off and covered him. He mumbled that he loved her just before he passed out. She hadn't noticed that there was a balcony in the room because it had been covered by a curtain. Marian surmised that the maid must have opened it when she turned down the room. She opened the door and walked outside. Their room was high enough so that she could see what she presumed was the Mississippi River as the sun was setting. The sun was reflecting off of some lingering dark clouds and it looked like the clouds were aflame. She had no paper so she tried to remember exactly how it looked so she could write about it someday. There was a sound she couldn't discern coming from the room. When she stepped back in she saw that Nathan was yelling in his sleep and appeared to be almost crying. She lay down next to him and put her hand on his chest and stroked it. He seemed to calm down, so she went and took off her clothes and washed her face and then laid back down next to him. She hoped he was in a better place tomorrow. Despite what she suspected would be an abysmal hangover, she wanted to get the real story about work. She suspected he might have been fired because of the way he had been acting but didn't want to press him just yet. There was also the book tour. Who knows how he would react to that, but that would have to wait as well. If there was one thing she had learned about marriage, it was that you had to ration information and know when to share it. She now understood why her mother used to tell her to not burden her father with *news*.

16

maryland

1980

The seemingly endless and barren New Jersey Turnpike finally gave way to the Delaware River. The bridge was the point in the drive home when Nathan felt the pull of his family. Delaware was a wisp of a state and he would be in Maryland soon. Where was Marian today? He had spent a week laying around in his underwear and decided that he wanted to go home. The last time he was home was when his little brother graduated from high school in June. His mother wanted to know when she was going to be a grandmother, though she insisted they come up with another designation for her that didn't make her feel so old. Marian had waited for him to answer and he just brushed his mother off by telling her they were having too much fun in New York.

He knew his mother would want to know what he was doing home and why Marian was on a book tour without him. His mother's view of marriage was that when you said "I do," you were signing up to be a Siamese twin. He had toyed with various explanations on the drive and had settled on telling her that he had to take vacation time before the end of the year or lose the time. Since his mother had never worked for a corporation, he figured she would accept whatever he said. Marian was sure to be surprised that he was at his mother's house. He would have to call her tonight and come up with some excuse. He wasn't sure he had put on a convincing performance in New Orleans about quitting his job, but she hadn't pressed him. Marian usually bided her time and didn't wade into conflict without knowing all the angles.

His parents lived in a small town of about five thousand that was just beyond the bedroom communities that surrounded the District of Columbia. Since his mother never worked and his father earned a modest salary working for the federal government, they didn't venture very far. Nathan was finally able to break free when he went to college and coming home usually felt like some form of confinement. Yet, now, he knew he needed to escape the city, and for the first time in a while, he was looking forward to seeing his little burg.

Most of the town had been developed in the 1950s. As he turned off the county road into his town, he noticed for the first time that the houses were starting to show their age. Most of them had old cedar siding that needed to be replaced and yards that were overcrowded with trees that were threatening to swallow up the houses. It was a gray wintry day, which matched his mood. When he approached the street he grew up, he suddenly felt like he wasn't supposed to be there. While it took several years of geographical reorientation, he now thought of New York as his home rather than suburban Maryland. He wasn't sure when the transformation took hold, but now he felt a sense of dislocation when he returned home. He thought about turning around but realized how ridiculous that was. He continued and parked in front of his childhood home. It looked like as if no one was there since there was no car in the driveway. His mother had been driving the same station wagon since before a man had walked on the moon. There was a NASA sticker on the bumper from the days when his father had worked there. Nathan got out of the car and went and sat on the porch, which clearly needed a new coat of paint. He pulled up some chips that were sticking up and threw them onto the lawn, which was now mostly brown after a brutally hot summer.

After a few minutes Nathan looked up the street and decided to walk over to the Meyer's house. Their daughter Carly had been his first "girlfriend" in seventh grade. She had developed in fifth grade and it had taken Nathan a few years before he was no longer intimidated by her physique. They had spent some time in her basement in the dark while he would fumble around with her bra, kiss her, and masturbate later in the shower at home. Mrs. Meyer happened to be opening her door when he walked by.

"Is that you Nathan?"

"It is."

"You are more handsome than ever. Come up here and give me a hug."

Nathan obeyed and Mrs. Meyer, who smelled of lavender, gave him a warm embrace.

"Carly would be so happy to see you. What brings you home? You're married now, right?"

"I am. A few years. How is Carly?"

"She's okay. She lives in an apartment in Columbia and works for a nice dentist over there."

"That's nice."

"She was married, but it didn't work out."

Nathan had heard the whole bloody story from his mother.

"Oh, sorry to hear that. How is Mr. Meyer?"

"He's fine. Thinking of retiring soon. You know we're at that age now, Nathan."

"Must be nice."

"There are advantages but, if I could wave a magic wand, I wouldn't mind being your age." She gave him a wistful look.

"Well, I don't want to keep you."

"Oh, not at all. Hey, let me give you Carly's number. I'm sure she would love to hear from you while you're in town." Mrs. Meyer disappeared into the house and came out with a slip of paper with her daughter's phone number. Her hand was shaking.

"Here."

"Thanks. Great to see you."

Nathan walked back to his mother's house and looked at the paper with Carly's number on it. He hadn't thought about her in years, but he was surprised she was already divorced. He put the paper in his pocket and it occurred to him that his mother left a key under the mat in the back of the house for emergencies. He wondered if it was still there and walked around the back to see that the yard had not been mowed in a few months. He looked under the mat and there was the key with some ants crawling over it. He brushed off the ants and went to open the front door. He felt a little strange opening it but, as the familiar scene washed over him, he felt like a little boy. He walked over to the mantle by the fireplace and looked at the dusty gallery of pictures. As the oldest child, he was prominently featured in most of them. His mother had crammed a new picture of his brother in his cap and gown on the end next to his wedding picture. Marian looked back at him with that shy smile of hers clutching a bouquet of roses. He wondered if she was signing books or reading one of her poems to a rapt audience of Midwesterners.

Nathan went out back and opened the shed. The mower looked like it hadn't been serviced in years but he was pleasantly surprised that he was able to power it up. He couldn't just leave that backyard looking like the Serengeti. By the time his mother followed the sound of the mower to the backyard, Nathan had just about completed his mission.

"Don't think you're getting an allowance." His mother smiled broadly. "What a nice surprise. What are you doing here?"

Although her smile suggested she was happy to see him, he could see her eyes carefully held a hint of concern.

"I was concerned about the lawn. You could have hidden a body back here." Nathan made a funny face.

"With good reason. Your father made me stop paying the Blackburn boy up the block and said he would do it."

"I think it's time to bring him back. Let me finish and I'll come in."

"Is Marian lurking about somewhere?"

"No, she is probably in St. Louis by now. Book tour." Nathan started the mower up to cut off any further conversation but he knew there would be more inquiries. After he returned the mower to what would undoubtedly be its final resting place one day, he tried to clean himself up. His mother was waiting like a recoiled panther as he walked in and immediately hugged him after he pulled off his coat.

"You're a sweaty mess. Did you bring extra clothes?"

"Not much. I only planned on staying one night."

"I can wash these. Why don't you change?"

Nathan went to the car to grab his duffel bag and ran inside to take a shower. His old room hadn't changed much. His baseball trophies were still there, along with all his Cardinals paraphernalia and posters of Musial and Gibson. His mother used to refer to his room as "the shrine" and he could see why. He opened his desk and spied some old concert tickets from a Crosby, Stills & Nash concert he had gone to when he was a junior in high school. He recalled how he and his friends had smuggled some beer into his friend's car that night and were half in the bag by the time the concert began. Some girls at the concert shared a few joints with them, which was the first time he had gotten high. He took a shower and changed. His mother was waiting in the kitchen with turkey sandwiches.

"You hungry? You had a long drive."

"Sure. Thanks."

"So, I may not work, but I do know it's Monday."

"I'm taking some vacation time. Have to use it now or lose it."

"I see. And Maryland is paradise in November?"

"I thought you would be happy to see me."

"I am of course. Just curious."

"I figured I haven't been home for a while."

"Everything okay with you and Marian?"

"Fine. Good."

"I saw her book in the bookstore downtown. I was very proud to purchase it, even if I can't follow some of it."

"It's not a Ludlum novel, Mom."

"Yes, I know smarty pants. How is work? The advertising world?"

"Good. Busy."

"So, your father won't be home for a few hours. He'll be surprised. He misses you."

"He does?"

"Of course. We both do."

"You call. He doesn't."

"He's not a caller. That's just him. During baseball season he follows your Cardinals."

"I didn't know that."

"He'll say something like, *Nathan's Cards won last night.*"

"I didn't know."

"It's tough on him. His boys are both gone now. You guys were his main companions. What do I know about sports and politics?"

"I guess I should call him more often."

"I'm sure he'd like that."

"I saw Mrs. Meyer."

"You did?"

"I took a walk. She told me Carly was divorced."

"She married some bum who cheated on her. I haven't seen her in a long time. You know Mr. Meyer had cancer last year?"

"I didn't know."

"Seems okay now, but he lost a lot of weight."

"That's too bad."

"Are you going to see her while you're home? I'm sure she'd love to see you."

"I doubt it."

Nathan ate his sandwich. After, he decided to take a ride into town and buy a book or some other reading material. The downtown was just a cluster of stores that ran for about a half mile and the only place that sold books was the old pharmacy. He picked up the latest John LeCarre novel and was greeted as he exited the store by a guy he used to play with in Little League.

"Nathan. Wow! Long time."

"Michael. Hey, how are you?"

"Good. Married. One kid on the way."

"You live around here?"

"I live a few blocks from my parents."

"Oh."

"You? You went to college, right?"

"Yeah. I'm living in New York now."

"The big city. Sweet. You married?"

"I am. About two years."

"Kids?"

"Not yet."

"You a lawyer or something?"

"Unemployed actually. I was in advertising."

"Smart guy like you will be fine."

"Yeah."

"Well, it was good seeing you. I need to get back to work."

"Take care."

Nathan watched as he walked away and entered one of the stores near the end of the main drag. He wasn't sure why he told Michael he was unemployed. He *was* tired of lying and it was sort of freeing to tell the truth. He had no job. His wife was the breadwinner and she didn't even make that much money from her books. At least, not yet. He walked by the store that Michael had entered and saw that it was an appliance repair shop. Nathan went back to his car and searched his pocket for the piece of paper with Carly's number. Maybe he would call her when he got back to his mother's house.

～

She was more attractive and taller than he remembered. It was Monday night, so she had to be a little tired after working all day, but you would have never known it. Nathan sat down at the table in the restaurant she had suggested, and thought the ambience was a bit too romantic, which made him feel guilty after she hugged him and sat down. Carly was wearing lipstick which Marian typically eschewed and had probably last applied on their wedding day.

"If a bolt of lightning had hit me today, it would have been less unexpected than your call. I think I said that right." She laughed and he saw she still had a little space between her two front teeth.

"This whole trip has been a bit spur of the moment."

"So, I hear you're living in New York."

"I am."

"So, I guess you're glad you left Dodge."

"I couldn't stay here." Nathan wasn't sure if he had offended her.

"I knew you'd never stay. You always seemed out of place here."

"I did?"

"Definitely. You were always talking about everything that was going on. Like you needed to see it for yourself. Did you?"

"Some. I went all over Europe and Asia. Not always glamorous, but worth it."

"Did you go with your wife?"

Nathan wasn't sure if they were going to avoid discussing marriage.

"I did. On one of the trips."

"I'm jealous. That must have been so romantic."

"Sometimes. It seems like so long ago. Have you ever travelled?"

"Not overseas. Alan. He was my husband. We went on a few trips. Florida. Camping in Virginia. Nothing too exotic."

"Well, you should travel more. There are so many incredible things to see."

"Your face lights up when you talk about it."

"It does? I guess I need to get back out there."

"You sound like my mother. She says I need to get back out there too. Only she's talking about dating. The problem is around here I'm not sure where *there* is."

"Pretty girl like you should easily find someone."

"That's sweet. You always were charming. There have been a few patients that asked me out, but it felt a little strange. Not sure my boss would like it."

"He doesn't need to know."

"I don't know. I need my job. So what kind of work do you do?"

"I'm in advertising. Not very exciting."

"Sounds cool. Any products I would know?"

"Yeah, I'm sure. Aspirin. Detergents. Beer. Other stuff."

"You don't sound so excited."

"It can be fun. I get to use my imagination. But I would be lying if I said it stirred my soul."

"Did you really think you would be doing something that stirred your soul?"

"Don't we all?"

"How many people get that chance?"

"I guess you're right. When did you get so wise?"

"A broken heart will give you lots of wisdom."

"I'm sorry."

"You didn't do it. I didn't give you the chance." Carly broke into a grin.

"Is that how you remember it?"

"We were young and stupid. Whatever happened, happened. You know?"

"I like that."

Nathan had already eaten his mother's turkey sandwiches, but he didn't want to be impolite so he had most of a second dinner. For an hour and a half, he forgot he was unemployed, married, and living in a six hundred square foot apartment. In her eyes he was the impossibly charming and adorable boy who was going to come home triumphant one day. Maybe they would name a street in his honor. He almost told her he had no job, but he couldn't bring himself to puncture her inflated view of him.

At the end of their dinner he walked her to her car and, to his surprise, she invited him back to her apartment. He didn't answer at first, and then he heard himself telling her that he would in another place and time. She leaned over and kissed him gently on the cheek and they hugged and then parted. He walked back to his car and stood next to it for a minute and watched her drive off. He didn't want to be *that* guy. He wanted to be the guy that Carly saw in that restaurant. He just had to find him.

17

detroit

Marian found herself waking up almost every night and turning on the television downstairs. She didn't need that complicated remote anymore because the television was now tuned to that channel with all the chefs. There was a seafood paella the chef with the bleached blonde hair made that she wanted to try and replicate. When Mira called the other night to ask her how she was enjoying the television, Marian was too embarrassed to tell her about the cooking shows, so she just said it was gathering dust. She felt guilty because she could hear the disappointment in Mira's voice.

This morning she was awakened by the ringing of a phone. The television was still on and there was a commercial for a blender. She began to realize that she had fallen asleep on the couch and the kitchen phone was ringing. Before she made it to the kitchen it stopped ringing and the answering machine clicked on.

"Marian. Hope I didn't wake you. I'm an early riser these days. This is Charles Norman. I hope you don't mind that I tracked you down. I was hoping we could meet for tea again sometime. I enjoyed our conversation. My number is 526-6598. I look forward to hearing from you."

Marian was frozen in place as she listened to the message and realized as she took a step forward that her heart was racing. *How did he get my number? I can't believe he called. What do I do now?*

1980

By the time Marian's book tour wound its way to Detroit, she was ready to see a friendly face. There were moments when she would read one of her poems and she would connect with someone in her audience. But those moments were fleeting and almost too intimate to share with total strangers. So when she looked up after she finished one of her poems and saw her mother sitting there rapt with one of her books in her hand, she felt like weeping. When she had thanked the readers for coming and waded through the crowd, she desperately wanted to hug her right there in public. Yet, she knew that was a sentiment her mother would find uncomfortable so she just walked up to her and waited. She wasn't sure, but she thought she saw tears in her mother's eyes.

"You came."

"You didn't think I'd come to see my daughter, the author?"

"It's a long drive," Marian offered to make sure her mother's feelings wouldn't be hurt.

"I find I like to drive now. Your father used to do all the driving and I didn't realize how much I missed it."

They were interrupted by the proprietor of the store who came over to thank Marian for coming. She felt her mother watching her and she was a little girl all over again hoping that she said the appropriate thing.

"He seems nice."

"Everyone's nice when you first meet them mother."

"Not everyone. Are you hungry?"

"You're asking me? You just drove four hours. Let's go back to my hotel. We can get something to eat there."

Her mother was still driving her father's old gray Cadillac with the bench seat in front. The seat was so comfortable and there was so much leg room in front, she felt like she was reclining in a living room. Marian offered to drive, took the keys from her mother and slid into the driver's seat. She could hear her father's booming voice call out whenever they reached their destination. "Ladies, we have arrived." She could see the worn places on the steering wheel where her father's hands used to rest. He rarely let her drive his precious car so this was indeed an unexpected treat. An hour ago she was sharing intimate thoughts with strangers and here she was communing with her father's spirit in his old Cadillac. Her mother was holding her copy of the book in her lap looking like the cat who swallowed the canary. Marian could see that her emotions were swirling as her grown up daughter drove her through the city.

The hotel restaurant looked like it was between meals and it took them a few minutes to gain someone's attention. The woman told them they were early for dinner, but said they could eat at the bar. They went and sat on bar stools, which amused

Marian. Her mother had probably never sat on a stool to eat, much less sat at a bar to have a meal. She looked completely out of place trying to find a place for her hands.

"I don't like these stools. So uncomfortable."

"You're just not used to it."

"Well, if they want you to sit here longer and drink they should have padded chairs."

"Interesting idea. I think after a few drinks you sort of forget where you're sitting. Anyhow, you could have told me that you were coming when we spoke before I left on the book tour."

"Now what fun would that be?"

"You? Fun?"

"Marian Elizabeth. Are you implying I'm not fun?"

"You're a barrel of laughs, mother." Marian smiled and turned to the bartender who asked for their orders.

"Your father would have been so proud of you."

"You sure about that?"

"Of course." Her mother said emphatically.

"I don't recall him ever reading a book. *The Wall Street Journal*, yes. Books, no."

"Just because he didn't read books doesn't mean he wouldn't have been proud of his daughter publishing a book of poetry?"

"Okay. So, are you ever going to get a new car?"

"It still works."

"Hanging on to the past?"

"I don't think so. Actually, speaking of the past, there is something I wanted to talk with you about."

"Okay."

"I met someone."

"You met someone?"

"Yes, a man."

"I assumed that part."

"Don't be fresh. He's a very nice man. I met him at church. He lost his wife a few years ago."

"So, what are you saying?"

"I just wanted you to know. I'm not sure what will happen, but he makes me very happy."

The child in Marian wanted to tell her mother she wasn't allowed to meet anyone or shack up with some strange man who wasn't her father. But she knew her mother was sharing with the adult Marian, so she resisted the urge to say something needlessly petulant.

"Wow. That's nice Mother."

Her own voice sounded very shrill and unnatural. She hoped her mother didn't notice.

"You sure?"

"Sure, why not? It's been, what, eight years since Daddy is gone. I think the statute of limitations has long since passed."

"I'd like you to meet him. His name is Christopher. You probably don't remember him. I was friendly with his wife, Grace."

"Is that odd for you?"

"At first. But he's such a lovely man. I know you'll like him."

"I'm sure I will."

"I was wondering if you could come to our house for Christmas this year. I know this is not my turn to make Christmas, but I really want you to meet him. If you can't, I'll understand. Maybe you could come after the New Year."

"I don't know mother. I'll have to speak with Nathan."

"Okay. So how is Nathan?"

"He's fine."

"Old married couple?" Her mother smiled.
"Something like that."
"How's his job?"
"Good, I guess. He doesn't talk about it much."
"I thought he was the chatty one between the two of you."
"Usually."
"To be honest I wasn't sure how you would handle all that public speaking today. I guess I still see you as that little girl who sat on the floor and played quietly with her dolls for hours."
"Where are those dolls?"
"The attic I suppose."
"Don't throw them out. You never know when I might need them."
"They're not going anywhere."
Their food arrived and they ate quietly. Marian insisted her mother stay the night with her at the hotel. There was only one bed and her mother wanted to sleep on the couch. Marian told her they were sleeping together and her mother relented. They watched some mindless television programs together for a few hours, and then Marian went to wash her face. When she walked back into the room her mother was on the phone saying goodnight to someone. Marian gave her a tee shirt to wear to bed and her mother washed up. A few minutes after she got in bed Marian spoke:
"Are you getting married?"
Her mother was silent for a few seconds.
"Would that upset you?"
"No. But that's why you want me to come home, isn't it?"
"No. It's just important to me that you meet him. I wouldn't marry him unless I knew you were okay with it."

"You're funny mother. You have my permission. Whenever the blessed event occurs."

Her mother turned the light on. She had tears in her eyes. Marian sat up and her mother put her arms around her and Marian tried to hold back her tears.

"You must really be happy."

"I am. He *really* loves me."

The emphasis didn't escape Marian's attention. She knew her mother had waited forever to have someone tell her she was loved.

"Of course, he does. I love you, too."

Her mother's eyes were welling up again. She leaned down and shut out the light to lay down again. She searched for Marian's hand and held it tightly.

18

christmas

1980

*M*arian wasn't sure how Nathan could possibly see the road as snow was enveloping their car. She had to close her eyes because the flakes flying at them as they drove were hypnotizing and the sensation started to make her a little unsteady. Nathan didn't really explain why he had travelled to Maryland while she was away. She assumed he was lonely. But it did make it easier for her to ask if they could go visit her mother for Christmas. Her mother rarely asked her for anything, so she really wanted to deliver after they bonded on her book tour.

She wasn't really sure how she felt about her mother remarrying. It wasn't something she ever really contemplated. Maybe it was her own childish desire, but for some reason, she figured her mother's memories would be enough for her. In retrospect, maybe she was naive to think that would be the case. Nathan didn't really react when she told him about the engagement, which was further evidence of the depth of the funk that he had slipped into. Nathan was always a romantic and the news of her mother's new love would have ordinarily reinforced his optimistic worldview. "Wow, that's nice," was about all he could muster. Marian hoped he was more like himself at her mother's house or she was sure to be questioned about the state of her marriage. Maybe her mother would be so giddy over their arrival that she wouldn't pick up on his mood. Nathan was usually able to turn on the charm whenever it was required.

She didn't realize that she had fallen asleep until Nathan was shaking her.

"Where are we? Gas station?"

"I can't see any more so I stopped at a motel."

"Do you know where we are?"

"I would say a few hours from your mother's house, give or take."

"She's going to be disappointed if we don't make it tonight."

"I'm happy you and your mother found some common ground, but I can't safely drive if I can't see."

"I know. You're right."

Nathan pushed open his door as the snow swept in, and Marian watched as he made his way to the door of the motel and disappeared. She suddenly had a terrible thought. What if he decided to make a clean sweep of it? What if he was so miserable that she was part of the problem and didn't know it? As far as she knew, he had only cheated on her that one summer when they were dating. She had never pressed him on why he'd betrayed her. At the time she felt like she was exhibiting strength, but sometimes she wondered if it was cowardice.

When he got back, she realized that she had to call her mother and tell her they weren't coming. As soon as they got in the room, she called her mother, who seemed relieved that they wouldn't be driving into the teeth of the snowstorm. She said it had been snowing for three or four hours and it was already a foot deep on the front porch. When she got off the phone, Nathan was starting to shake on the bed as he slipped into sleep, clearly exhausted from stressful hours at the wheel in poor weather. Bored, Marian looked around the room for the first time. Brown curtains hung above the streaky window that looked out onto the parking lot. They were partially open so Marian got up and to close them. She looked out and saw that their car was already covered with a few inches of snow. Another car was pulled up next to theirs and Marian watched as a little girl in a bright pink coat got out of the car along with her father. The little girl stopped and craned her head and stuck out her tongue so she could taste the snowflakes. When her father realized that his daughter wasn't behind him, he called to her, but she was too busy turning her sneakers into snowshoes and sliding along the parking lot surface. The sight of the little girl cheered her up momentarily. Smiling, she closed the curtains and went to undress. Marian found herself noticing children more often these days. It was almost like they were suddenly in Technicolor while the rest of the world was in black and white, like scenes from the *Wizard of Oz*. She imagined someone had somehow secreted her away and brainwashed her, like Frank Sinatra in the *Manchurian Candidate*, so that she would fall in love with every child she saw. She hadn't shared anything to Nathan because she didn't want to pressure him right now, but she knew she would eventually feel compelled to reveal her burgeoning desire to have a child.

There was a crappy little television in the room, but she didn't want to wake Nathan. Plus, she didn't really watch much television anyhow, so she fished around in her suitcase for her writing pad and pen to begin jotting notes. The next thing she heard was the sound of a squealing tire and that's when she realized it was morning and Nathan wasn't next to her anymore. She had slept through the night. At some point, Nathan had awakened and was in the process of trying to free their car. He came in a few minutes later bringing with him bright sunlight and frigid air.

"Close the door." Marian shielded her eyes.

"Sorry."

"When did you get up?"

"A while ago. I must have fallen asleep pretty early."

"A few seconds after we got here."

"It stopped snowing. Finally."

"I was thinking about your mother."

"What were you thinking?"

"She probably hadn't given a second thought to life without your father and then he's gone just like that. She probably went into some sort of hibernation and then this man comes along and the long sleep is over and life starts anew. Or something like that."

"Sounds like I've rubbed off on you. Very poetic." Marian was so moved by his description that she wanted to kiss him.

"Why don't you come over here?"

Nathan took the hint and finished taking off his clothes. Marian slipped off her pajama bottoms and they made love.

Marian barely moved as she surrendered herself to him and she could feel that he was emotionally raw. She couldn't be sure, but she thought he might have started crying. He had buried his face in the pillow. When they were done, she draped herself on him.

His breathing slowed and he said, "I was fired."

"I had a feeling. Why didn't you want to tell me?"

"Pride, I guess. Maybe it's for the best. I've been floating along for a while. I just figured nobody noticed. I was wrong."

"We'll figure it out. Maybe it's time for *you* to come out of hibernation." Marian lifted up her head from his chest and made sure he could see her smiling. He leaned down and kissed her on the cheek.

"Maybe."

Nathan wanted to say something about what he had read in her journal this morning, but he decided it wasn't the right time. He could see from what she had written last night that children were on her mind, but he knew he wasn't ready to be a parent. Not when he didn't even know what he wanted to do next. He hoped she would understand.

19

seattle

*M*ira was only two blocks from her mother's house and could feel her anxiety level rising. It had been over a year since her father had passed away unexpectedly. How long was she supposed to put her life on hold? Her boyfriend Matt was threatening to leave and move to Seattle without her. She kept putting him off with her sob story that her mother was alone and couldn't bring herself to leave her while she was grieving. But she knew the time was drawing to a close when emotional blackmail would hold him in New York.

The light changed and she drove past her childhood friend Elizabeth's house. As with most of her high school friends, she had lost contact with her during college. She just wasn't very good at staying in touch with people. The neighborhood was now dominated by young families with children that were knocking down or expanding the modest split-level houses until some were unrecognizable monstrosities. She wondered how long her mother would stay in that empty house by herself. She had her precious garden in the backyard, but she lived with a ghost now. Her mother was never a social butterfly and, as far as she could tell, she rarely left the house except to get food and new pads to write on. Was she too obvious with the television? Did her mother sense she might be compensating for something? Maybe it didn't matter at this point.

Mira parked in front of the house and watched her mother puttering around in the backyard through a rusted gate. Her parents had not spent much money beautifying the interior of their house, but her mother had insisted on creating a garden that reminded her of some gardens she had seen on her treks around Europe. Her mother straightened up when she heard her coming.

"Well. Surprise, surprise."

"The garden looks good. The gate not so much."

"You can tell how much I'm not writing by how good it looks." She ignored the gate comment.

"Not writing much, huh?"

"Fits and starts. Did my agent put you up to this?"

"No. But I did want to speak to you about something."

"That sounds ominous."

"No. Nothing like that. But you know I told you that Matt wants to live on the West Coast, right?"

"Not sure I recall that, but okay. So, you're leaving me?"

"I'm not leaving anyone. I'm just thinking about moving."

Marian knew she sounded like a terrible mother, but she wasn't prepared for this.

"Poor choice of words. Is this what you want?"

"For now, yes. I'm happy with him."

"What about your job here?"

"I'll find another one. Retail is retail, Mom. I'm not you."

"What does that mean?"

"I'm not in love with what I do. It doesn't define me. I wasn't that lucky."

"You sound like your father."

"Daddy's little girl. Isn't that what you always said?"

"You two were as thick as thieves."

Mira wanted to forestall any discussion about her father or her mother since that would draw her back into her mother's life with ghosts.

"So, you enjoying the television?"

"I have to confess I do sort of like that channel with all the cooking shows."

"It is addictive."

"So when are you planning on leaving?"

"I'm not sure. We need to find a place to live. It's not like I'm never coming back."

There was something about the tone in Mira's voice that reminded her of the way Nathan and her father could make her feel helpless.

"Don't worry about me. I met someone," she blurted out and immediately regretted her revelation.

"You did?"

"Well, yes."

"That man. From the cemetery?"

"Yes. We had a lovely time at the tea shop in town."

Marian put it out there and couldn't turn back now.

"Wow. I mean, that's great Mom."

"So, I'll be okay. My life isn't over."

"I never said it was."

"Not exactly. Anyhow, let me know if I can help you with your move. I don't see Matt doing much packing."

"He helps."

"Well, I'm around if you need something. Unless, I'm out with Charles."

"Charles."

"That's his name."

"I got that. Well, I'll have to meet him before I leave."

"You did meet him."

"I met him, but I didn't know he was soft on my Mom or I would've had a lot more questions." Mira smiled.

Questions. That is exactly why she never should have said anything. Mira thought she was her mother now.

"You know all you need to know right now. Are you staying for dinner?"

"No, I'm meeting some friends for drinks."

Marian figured now she could race home and tell her boyfriend with the pony tail that she was free at last.

"Sounds like a plan. Have fun."

"Okay. Bye mom."

Mira gave Marian a hug and she could tell her mother hadn't brushed or washed her hair in a few days. She wondered if the whole Charles story was concocted on impulse for her benefit. She walked down the driveway to her car, paused and looked back. The house was really starting to show its age. The paint on the shutters was fading and the screen door needed to be replaced. She wondered if her neighbors were counting the days until the funny lady with the overgrown English garden finally was going to leave or kick off. Her mother had left the neighborhood socializing to her father. She hoped she was wrong and her mother was seeing Charles regularly. She wasn't even sure what that would look like or how it would make her feel, but she was going to be three thousand miles away and someone else would have to step up to the plate. Why did you leave dad?

20

metz

1990

$\mathcal{N}$athalie's father Stefan didn't say it explicitly, but it was clear that he considered himself more German than French. He went on about his Germanic ancestry as if it was something others should admire him for, a badge of honor maybe. He always took them, without fail, to his favorite German restaurant in Metz so they were all forced to imagine the Nazis had not been driven out of France. Charles wasn't sure if the American troops had been involved in liberating Metz, but he wondered if her father saw him as the embodiment of all those meddlesome Americans who had liberated Europe. When Charles would gently express his feelings to Nathalie, she would laugh and tell him that the war was a long time ago and he was making too much of her father's *fanfaronades*. He didn't know if she was brushing him off to avoid the subject, or if she really didn't see that her father was boasting because he had never really accepted his new country.

As the children got a little older, their annual trips to Metz got a little more tolerable. Nathalie's parents focused on their grandchildren, and he could avoid talking with Stefan. Much to his chagrin, Stefan had developed a bond over the years with Henry in particular. Charles tried to grin and bear it. He told himself it was only ten days a year, and he knew that those trips would break the fever that seemed to burn every year when Nathalie began to miss France.

He wasn't sure if it was because he still felt jet lagged, but this evening Stefan seemed particularly insufferable. He was making himself laugh loudly talking about some accident he had seen that day, which made little Henry laugh along with him. Charles watched as Stefan's bulbous cheeks grew redder and he kept slapping the table so hard the silverware was jumping. He hadn't said anything really offensive, but Charles didn't like that his son was chuckling at someone's misfortune. The third time Stefan laughed and Charles slammed his fist on the table.

"Enough!"

Everyone looked at Charles who hadn't planned on making a scene.

"Charles." Nathalie said and made an irritated face.

"They don't laugh in your country?" Stefan said derisively.

With a withering look, Nathalie begged him to not respond. Charles wanted to hold back. He really did.

"Not at the expense of others. We're not callous."

"Callous? What is this word?"

Henry looked at his father with a quizzical look on his face. Kristin, who was almost twelve, looked like she wanted to slip under the table. Charles could feel his heart begin to resume its normal rhythm.

"It's not important."

"Okay, smart guy."

The remainder of the dinner was a silent minuet of forks and spoons and muted conversation. Charles knew Nathalie was going to be furious with him, but part of him didn't really care. He had stifled his desire to tell him off for years. Outside the restaurant he wasn't surprised when Henry jumped into his grandfather's car. Nathalie decided they should walk the streets and take in some of the nightlife. Despite Nathalie's father, Charles thought the city was charming with its soaring Gothic cathedrals and meticulous gardens. They found a quaint café that served crepes. Kristin grasped his hand as they walked past strangers enjoying the cool breeze of the late summer evening. Unlike when she was younger, Kristin and Charles did not have much physical contact anymore except when they were in cities or traveling. She seemed to still seek the comfort of his hand and he didn't dare look at her for fear she would unhook herself. After an hour of roaming the streets, they headed back to the car. He was still waiting for their negative reaction to his behavior at the restaurant. Nathalie held her fire and let Kristin have at him when they closed the car doors.

"Why were you picking on Grandpa Stefan tonight? He just likes to laugh."

"At the wrong things, at the wrong times."

"Who cares? He's old and jolly."

"I thought you were the queen of propriety?"

"Proper you mean?"
"Yes, something like that."
"Mom."
"I'm not discussing this now. You and your brother need to get ready for bed when we get back to grandpa's house."

Nathalie was surprisingly quiet in their bedroom while she slipped off her clothes. Was she giving him the silent treatment? That wasn't a weapon she had ever used in their relationship. She settled into bed and turned to him.

"Did you see the street theater near the restaurant? I want to go back there tomorrow night."

"You think the kids will like that?"
"Sure. Why not?"
"I don't know."
"Don't you *see* all this city has to offer us?"
"Offer us? We've been here how many times? I think I've seen it all."
"I want to move back here."
"What?"
"I don't like suburbia. There is no street life where we are. Don't you see the life here? The people on the streets? It's alive."

He wanted to say with a lot of old Germans but he didn't think she would be interested in humor right now.

"We have New York very close by. We can go there anytime."

"Yes, but we don't live there, it's not the same. We don't *participate* in that place like we would here. How long did it take for us to get home? Fifteen minutes? We could be part of something."

Charles kept thinking of her father's belly heaving up and down as he laughed at the restaurant. He couldn't possibly live close to that man all year round.

"My business is in New York. That's how we survive as a family. It allows you to be home with them and paint."
"I don't have to paint. You can sell the business and start one here in France. You already have contacts here. Isabelle could help you. You know she adores you."
There was a knock at the door and Henry came running in. Nathalie put her arms out and Henry jumped into them.
"I don't like that room. It's too dark."
"But you have Kristin with you."
"She's mean."
"No, she's not. She just likes her own space and it's not possible here."
Ordinarily, Charles would have sent Henry back to his room, but he had no interest in continuing their conversation, so he was silent. Henry quickly fell asleep and Charles waited for a few minutes and picked him up and put him back in his room. Kristin was still awake reading a book and looked up.
"Do you like it here?" he asked.
"Metz?"
"Yes."
"It's pretty."
"Would you ever want to live here?"
"In Grandpa's house?"
"No. In Metz, as a family."
She thought about it for a few moments and he noticed that her nose was starting to become more prominent like her mother.
"I don't speak French or German."
"That's true. Don't worry about it. I was just curious."
"You think mom wants to move?"

"I don't know. I've never asked her."
"I'm sure she misses her parents."
"Like you would?" Charles grinned.
"Don't get crazy."
"Good night."

By the time he returned to his bedroom Nathalie was snoring lightly. She was almost forty, but her skin was so flawless she looked ten years younger. What if the fever didn't break this time and she insisted on moving to France? Could he possibly live without her? Could he eat dinner with that man every week while he guffawed at someone's misfortune? He had seven more days to endure in Metz. It seemed like an eternity.

21

scrapes

1985

*M*ira walked ahead of him as they approached the light on 79th street. There was a moment when he could barely see the red Cardinals baseball cap she was wearing and, then, she was gone. Nathan started to run and a few seconds later realized she had kneeled down to pet a Boxer that was sitting on the concrete enjoying the attention. The dog's owner was an attractive, raven-haired girl wearing a Columbia sweatshirt, who was kneeling to chat with Mira.

"Oh, hi." She broke into a wide smile and Nathan could see how adorable she was.

"I see you've met Mira."

"Mira. I love her name. Mira seems to have made a canine friend."

"Daddy, I want a dog. Can we get a dog?" Mira implored with a serious face.

"I don't know honey, we'll see."

"Boxers are great. They love kids."

"I'm sure they do. Thanks for letting her pet her."

"It's a he. Neville."

"History major?"

"How'd you know?" The girl smiled and college suddenly didn't seem a million miles away.

"Well, we have to get to the cleaners—"

"Caroline."

"Nice to meet you, Caroline. I'm Nathan."

"Nathan. Strong name. She's a cutie pie. How old is she? Four?"

"Good guess. Just turned."

"I'll let you two go. Come on Neville. Take care."

Mira waved goodbye to Caroline and Neville as Nathan watched her turn the corner.

"You can't run ahead of me, Mira. You almost gave daddy a heart attack." Nathan immediately regretted the remark.

"What's a heart attack, daddy?"

"You just scared daddy. You need to stay close to me on the streets, okay?"

"Okay."

Nathan decided he didn't want to go to the cleaners after all. He didn't feel like dragging all those clothes back home, so they headed towards the playground. The aborted trek to the cleaners was only a pretense for getting out anyway. He just needed to escape the apartment. Mira's toys seemed to grow exponentially by the week and the space, his space, seemed to be getting more and more cramped. Mira was excited about the change in plans and held Nathan's hand during the entire walk to the playground as her part of the bargain. He looked down at Mira as they walked and wondered if she would think her father was a monster for making her don a baseball cap instead of a pink bow. She didn't seem to mind, even though he couldn't seem to interest her in watching baseball on television. At the hospital, when Marian had asked him if he was disappointed, they were having a girl instead of a boy. He had lied to her and said, "don't be silly." For some reason he had never considered they might have a girl. But when she started walking and talking he fell deeply under her spell. When he visited his parents for the first time with Mira, his mother took him aside and whispered in his ear. *You're in love, aren't you? You look so happy.* He didn't reply, but she was right. Mira had burned away the fog that had settled all around him and he was finally able to see the future more clearly. It was shortly after that revelation that he decided to go back to school to earn a master's degree so that he could teach history.

The playground was nothing like those he remembered growing up. It was mostly concrete, and it had a few lonely swings with rusting chains along with some beaten up slides and monkey bars. Accidents waiting to happen. None of that mattered to Mira who was fearless and careened down the slides and giggled when she was deposited at the bottom. Nathan had been standing near the swing and, by perhaps the tenth time she went down the slide, his attention wandered. He was watching a double-parked couple attempting to load a dining room table into a station wagon with no success. Before he could turn around Mira was tumbling like a ball of yarn on the concrete. Her baseball cap had flown off her head and she finally stopped a few feet away from him. A father who had been pushing his son on the swings came running over. Mira was dazed and on her back and Nathan quickly checked to see if she was bleeding and if she was in one piece. Luckily, it looked like just her knees were skinned. When Mira saw the look on Nathan's face she started wailing and he picked her up off the ground and held her. The man from the swings offered him some tissues which he used to dab her scrapes.

Mira was no lightweight anymore, but Nathan continued to carry her back to the apartment. He hoped Marian had awakened by now. He had left her sleeping after her late night with her old friends from Columbia. Mira had stopped crying by the time he made it into the brownstone, where he gingerly lowered her to the ground as she bounded inside looking for Marian. Since there were only two rooms in the apartment, he assumed she was still sleeping when there was no sign of her in the living room. He heard muffled sounds from inside the bedroom and then he made out his name being called. He walked into the bedroom and Marian was holding Mira and crying.

"It's just some scrapes. Nothing to cry about."

"I'm not crying about her knees."

Nathan quickly scanned his memory for something that he had done to elicit this reaction. Ellen.

"Um. Then what's wrong?"

"You know what's wrong."

"I do?"

"Ellen."

"Ellen?"

Nathan could feel his heart begin to accelerate and he felt lightheaded. What had Ellen told her?

"Don't."

Mira, who had been resting her head on Marian's shoulder, turned around and repeated the word *don't* to Nathan. Nathan was afraid to say anything for fear he would make it worse.

"Get out."

22

mirrors

*M*arian hadn't really looked in the mirror in quite some time. What was the point? She knew there were wrinkles and spots and other areas that no amount of time spent in the moisturizer and creams aisle would help. Even when she was much younger, when some might have looked her way given the right dress or lighting, it wasn't as if she spent an inordinate amount of time gazing at herself. Nathan saw something in her that she struggled to find, except on rare occasions.

It wasn't as if Charles had seen her all prettied up at the cemetery or tea shop. So, when she took a long look at herself, she wondered if it was worth using any of her neglected makeup or the expensive soaps Mira had bought her on Mother's Day a few years ago. She didn't say anything to Mira, but she had serious doubts soaps sporting exotic names purchased from some ritzy store at the mall were any more useful than the ones she bought on sale in the supermarket. She did look a bit pale so she surrendered and applied some blush. Then, plucked a few wayward eyebrow hairs before rummaging through her closet for something acceptable to wear. She had lost some weight over the past year and most of her nicer clothes seemed to just hang off her, ignoring the body underneath. While she couldn't decide if this benefited her or not, the clothes just didn't fit her very well.

Since she didn't think this meeting was going to lead to anything, she wasn't going to waste her time and money to buy something she might never wear again. A decision she now mildly regretted. So, she cobbled together an outfit that was more elaborate than the jeans and Nathan's oversized Bob Marley tee shirt she was wearing the last time they met. She even opted for dressier shoes which she hadn't worn in ages since she preferred the comfort of her far less constricting Birkenstocks.

Marian looked up at the clock and saw she was nearly out of time. Was she going because she told Mira she was dating someone, or because she really wanted to go? Perhaps there had been some part of that little white lie that had been wish fulfillment, but she wasn't sure how much. There was no turning back now since she had made the commitment, and he seemed so pleased when she agreed to meet him today. She prided herself on reliability, so she quickly walked out of the house to her car and slid into the front seat. She looked in the rear-view mirror at her face as a final check and saw herself in the back seat of her father's car. In the days before everyone wore seatbelts, she used to play with her mother's hair from behind. She wanted to see her mother more now that Nathan was gone. He had assumed the role her mother had filled so well for all those years, as the bulwark between her and her own insecurities that often sought to upend her. She had started a poem on the subject for her new book:

> *In the beginning*
> *there were monsters*
> *and ghosts*
> *under my bed*
> *and gorgons*
> *that rattled around my head*
> *mother*
> *slay them now*
> *so I can sleep*
> *so I can dream*
> *of little bo peep*

Marian was still working on the transition in the poem from mother to husband and trying to decide if she liked the rhyming when she glanced at her hand on the wheel. She was still wearing her wedding band. Should she take it off? If he had noticed that she was wearing it last time they met and saw that it was gone, then he might read too much into that. She wasn't looking to make any statements.

The tea shop was nearly empty, and Charles was already sitting at a table. He immediately got up and pulled her chair out. Marian couldn't recall the last time someone had been so polite.

"Glad you could make it." Charles said as he sat back down.

"Well, thank you for remembering me."

"I happen to like reggae." Charles smiled.

"Oh, my tee shirt last time. Nathan, my late husband was a big fan."

"Well, he had good taste." Marian wondered if he was referring to the music or her. She decided it was the music.

The waiter came over, and Marian allowed Charles to order tea for the both of them.

"You look nice."

"Oh. Thank you. You always seem to look nice."

Now she really felt like she was officially on a date. She could feel perspiration creep into her palms. She made a mental note to pick up her mug of tea carefully.

"I think it's an occupational hazard. I got used to all the sales meetings wearing my Sunday best. Hard habit to break."

"So how is the new book going?"

"To be honest, it's not too far along. I'm assuming you're not a spy for my new publisher." Marian winked.

"No ma'am. Scout's honor. But to be honest I don't quite understand how a writer who, I assume, must be inspired to write, can ever be asked to write according to someone's schedule, except her own."

"Do you want to be my agent?"

"Depends on my cut. I understand writers get paid and that work has to be produced and pitched to publishers, but it's an odd system. I'm can't say I have an alternative, since everyone needs money to live."

"Yes, even us writers. In all seriousness, I think it's a system built on trust, and when that trust breaks down, you're interfering with the artistic process."

"Can I ask what the subject of your new work is?"

"Something you might be familiar with. Loss."

"That I am. Have you been able to absorb it all enough to distill it into words?"

"I'm not so sure you absorb so much as you adapt, or try to adapt. Perhaps that's why I'm struggling to write this book. Even a year later, the last forty-five years is, as you say, not easy to distill."

"My daughter tells me I should write things down and my son tells me to walk out the door every day and look for my future. Who's right?"

"Maybe both?"

"I don't know. I'm not much of a writer. I've always been more of an action person."

"Is that why I'm here?" Marian smiled.

"That's why you're here. When you walked into the cemetery office I may have been grieving, but I could tell you were about to give that poor man a piece of your mind about your husband's grave, right?"

"Yes, and I felt like such a fool, to be honest. Misdirected anger and all."

"Even if your timing was off, your passion was admirable. I like passionate people. Always have. So, I guess that's why I'm sitting here with you."

"It's funny how sometimes you don't see yourself clearly, and then someone comes along and makes you see your better angels."

"I think I will take that as a compliment. Thank you."

Marian sat back and sipped her tea while the word "passion" flitted around in her head. She couldn't remember the last time she had been connected to that word in any way. She smiled back at Charles and took a sip from her tea. There was some undissolved sugar at the bottom of her cup and it made her last sip particularly sweet.

23

queens

1985

*M*artin's dog wanted to sniff every tree in Queens. When Nathan had asked if he could crash for a few days, he hadn't realized that Martin was probably figuring out how often he could prevail upon Nathan to walk his dog. When you weren't paying rent, it was kind of hard to tell your temporary landlord and savior that picking up dog shit was out of the question. His little Shih Tzu, Vincent, wouldn't move his bowels until he knew he had exhausted the entire universe of possibilities for staying outside one more minute. Strangely he could also sense when you were giving up on him, and then and only then would he relieve himself.

Given the parochial nature of New York City, Nathan didn't really know much about Queens and he wished he had remained blissfully ignorant of the outer borough. Queens seemed to be neither city nor suburb while commanding the least attractive features of both community forms. The Upper West Side may as well have been on Pluto it seemed so distant. There were no elegant buildings with doormen nor the meadows and gardens of Central Park. There were just garish storefronts with metal gates hovering in anticipation of closing time and streets pocked with litter that reeked of working-class resignation. There was a moment during the previous day's subway ride when he seriously considered going home to Maryland. But what would he tell his mother? Your little boy couldn't keep it in his pants? He couldn't bear to see his mother's disappointment. So, he decided that living away from his family was his penance. Banished to Queens. It sounded like the title of a bad theater production or worse, a TV sitcom. Perhaps the only saving grace was that he really liked Martin, who was the only gay person he knew who actually admitted to being gay. In faculty meetings at school, he could see some of the older teachers cringe when Martin opened his smart mouth, which made him like Martin even more.

Today marked two weeks since he had been thrown out of his apartment and Marian still wasn't picking up the phone. What must Mira be thinking? Who was picking her up from school? His mother usually waited to hear from him, but what if she called? He would have to call her soon. But what would he say? Maybe this would all be over soon.

Martin was home before him today, so luckily, he didn't have to walk the dog. It had been raining all day, which made him feel even more pathetic. Martin was parked on the couch sipping a glass of red wine with Vincent draped over his lap. Vincent looked up, barely, and wagged his tail.

"You've made quite an impression on Vincent."

"We're pals now. The pooper scooper law has seen to it."

"Want a glass?" Martin motioned to the bottle.

"Sure."

Nathan went to the kitchen and searched for a clean glass.

"Above the oven." Martin yelled behind him. Nathan found one and poured himself a generous glass and sat down on the purple easy chair across from Martin.

"Cheers. Tough day at school?"

"Not so bad. The kids were pretty tame today."

"I don't know how you teach history to sixth graders. Sounds dreadfully boring."

"They can be entertaining. And even enlightening from time to time."

"So no word from the home front?"

"Nope."

"I knew there was a reason I like men."

"Oh really? No drama with your boyfriends?"

"No. If you haven't figured it out yet, I'm more of the high maintenance type. So, I usually look for no drama boys."

"So, what are you doing out here in Queens?"

"On the edge of the known universe?" Martin cackled and Vincent looked up. "I guess you're not a fan?"

"If you like hardware stores, laundromats, and delis, it's a great place."

"Snob. Look at you, Mr. Upper West Side. It's cheaper here. I can crash in the city whenever I want to."

"So, what the hell am I going to do?"

"Beg?"

"I've never seen her so angry. I don't know. Maybe it's over." Nathan took a big gulp of his wine.

"Men and their dicks. It's a curse that's for sure."

"Is that supposed to help?"

"She's a poet, right? How about writing her a letter or something?"

"That's not actually a bad idea."

"See, I can be useful. Right, Vincent?" Vincent looked up and wagged his tail. Martin let him lick the bottom of his wine glass.

―

Marian lay in the dark waiting for her little girl to fall asleep. Had she talked as much as Mira? She didn't think so, but she would have to ask her mother. She finally heard the heavy breathing and then the phone started ringing in the kitchen. Marian didn't pick up the phone these days and waited for the answering machine to click on. It was Nathan again.

"Marian. Are you there? Marian? I miss you and Mira terribly. Are you there? Can you pick up? We have to talk about this. You know I love you. I hope you can forgive me for my stupidity someday. God, I hope so. I don't even know how it happened. Like I told you before, I'm at Martin's apartment. Please call me."

She was still too angry to speak with him. How could she have been so stupid and trusting? Since he had cheated on her in college, maybe she should have been looking for the signs, but what kind of way is that to live? The funny thing was she actually believed he did love her and Mira, but she was trying to square that determination with what occurred. Having lived through her parents' imperfect marriage, she wasn't expecting a seamless journey, but she had hoped to avoid any chasms. And now, here she was staring over the cliff. She looked over at Mira and saw Nathan in her sleeping face. She had his expressions and, luckily, his dimples. She seemed to have forgotten she had yelled at Nathan and just wanted to know when Daddy would be back "from his trip."

She lay there and contemplated the meaning of love and whether it could survive when one person took out a scissor and cut the invisible tether that bound a couple together. Could that string be pieced back together or was it irreparably damaged?

24

sacramento

*M*arian had never been much of a caller, so, when Nathan passed, she dreaded contacting some of her old friends. She expected that they would give her grief for losing touch. Her contact with most of them over the years was limited to exchanging Christmas cards. Luckily, the power of awful news seemed to tamp down most of the indignation. A few of them even surprised her and flew great distances to attend the funeral. Hilary, one of her college roommates, came all the way from Sacramento. Hilary had been brought into the apartment by one of the other girls. Since Marian was deep into the Nathan adventure at that point, she didn't see much of her, but she always thought she was a shy but sweet girl.

"You're probably wondering why I came all this way." Hilary had bluntly said to her after the last guests departed. She had invited her to stay overnight at the house given how far she had come, even though she really didn't want to deal with guests and secretly wished she had turned her down.

"I don't know. I guess I assumed you felt like we had some connection from college?"

Marian was a little surprised at how frank she was. This was not the Hilary she remembered, but college had been over forty years ago.

"When we were in college you probably remember how painfully shy I was. It took a lot of living and some lengthy therapy to come out of my self-imposed hibernation. But you never were condescending like so many of the other girls. Even though you had your boyfriend, you always made sure I was included in parties and events, even though you really barely knew me. Nathan didn't know me either, but he treated me the same way. He may have been the only guy I spoke to for any length of time in college. I never told you how much I appreciated it and over the years, there were many times I thought about college, and wish I did. So, when you called, I know you assumed I would politely decline, but I felt like I needed to come. I lost my husband a few years ago. Cancer. I thought maybe I could be a comfort to you in some way. I don't know."

Marian had not been expecting this confession and didn't immediately reply because she was still processing Hilary's words.

"You probably noticed I didn't cry much today. Family trait, unfortunately. But what you just said was so unexpected I—"

Hilary had been sitting across from her and got up and sat next to Marian who began to sob. Hilary held her and, after a few minutes, Marian regained control of herself. They ended up staying up half the night talking and, by the morning, a wholly unexpected and enduring friendship had been formed in the crucible of one of her darkest days.

When Hilary called to tell her she wanted to come for a visit,

Marian briefly wondered if Hilary could somehow sense when Marian needed her. Marian was uncomfortable with change. Her daughter was about to move away, leave her, and she had begun to date for the first time in over forty years. Hilary's visit was welcome, almost needed. The more surprising news was her declaration that she had gotten married a few weeks before to some man she had been dating for a while. Marian tried to take it in stride, but for some reason it threw her for a loop. She had asked Marian to pick her and her new husband up at the airport, and Marian agreed, even though she despised airports and their confusing signs and windy turns. Who could be expected to read all those signs while navigating off ramps, cars, buses, and pedestrians?

Luckily, she found the correct on ramp and squeezed herself between taxis and waited for Hilary. She hoped the airport police wouldn't shoo her away. When Hilary appeared a few minutes later she was walking next to a man with a speckled gray beard and dark horn-rimmed glasses. That was him. Marian honked and jumped out to greet Hilary who hugged her.

"How was your flight?"

"I don't like flying, but having this guy helped." Hilary put her hand on the man's shoulder.

"This is my husband, Roland." Marian tried to size up whether Roland belonged with her.

"Nice to meet you, Roland." Marian stuck out her hand which Roland shook.

"Likewise."

"Let's get in the car before one of these taxi drivers eats me for breakfast and you can regale me with all the wedding news in the car."

Marian didn't really like surprises because, to her, they were euphemisms for change. She had experienced enough change lately and Hilary's news just added to the pile. Since she knew virtually nothing about this man, she decided to make small talk on the drive back from the airport. She didn't know what he knew. He seemed pleasant enough, and Hilary was glowing, so who was she to rain on their parade? It just seemed like yesterday that Hilary was a lonely widow and now she was married. She assumed that these things happened at an accelerated pace when you got older, but how much could you really know about a person in a year or less? Did Charles expect her to move at that pace? She still barely knew him.

Fortunately, Roland was reasonably chatty and they eventually got around to discussing the matter of his biography. He insisted there wasn't much to tell. Divorced years ago. No children. Sales manager for a soda distributor until he retired last year. He admitted he had joined the hiking group hoping to meet someone. Hilary had caught his eye immediately, and blushed when he said this. For a moment, Marian saw the shy nineteen-year-old girl who used to tilt her head slightly so she wouldn't have to look you in the eye. After dessert, Roland said he was tired from the flight and gracefully allowed Marian and Hilary to have some time to catch up. Marian wondered if this was pre-planned. She made coffee and they sat in nearly the same positions as they had in the evening of the day that Nathan had been buried. Marian was surprised she remembered that detail. The days surrounding Nathan's death were lost in a blur of decisions, tears, and exhaustion.

"Okay, so I understand if you're angry with me for not telling you months ago about him," Hilary said.

"No, just a little puzzled."

"Look, I know what it's like grieving for someone, and I didn't want to throw this in your face."

"I would've been happy for you, but I appreciate your consideration of my feelings."

"You sure?"

"I'm sure. So, you're really married huh? Wow. Let me see that ring up close."

Hilary extended her hand across the coffee table and Marian showed the requisite interest in the diamond. Marian didn't have the heart to tell her she had no interest in jewelry.

"Very nice. He seems like a really good egg."

"He is. He's a very decent guy."

"So, you're happy? You look happy."

"Do I? I am. I definitely am. It's been long enough. Being alone, I mean."

"Sounds like it was a whirlwind."

"Yeah, it was pretty fast. I think Roland's been waiting a long time to find someone, so things moved pretty fast. I'm okay with it. I didn't want to lose him, you know?"

"Sure. I can see that."

"So, what about you? Anything new since we spoke last time?"

So she could buy time deciding how she wanted to share her news, Marian excused herself for a minute to pour the coffee into mugs and set down some pastries on the coffee table.

"Well, my Mira announced she's moving to Seattle. That was a bit of a blow."

"Seattle. Well, on the bright side, you can visit her and then come down to see me in Sacramento. Seattle's a great city by the way. Great seafood."

"I'm sure I'll do that. Still, I'm going to miss her. She doesn't appreciate how much."

"I'm sure she does, Marian. She going for work?"

"No, just love." Marian smiled ruefully. "I hope it's love. Her boyfriend wants to move there. I don't know why exactly. The seafood, maybe."

"Cute. Well, at least she won't be alone."

"I'm just a bitter old lady. He's okay. He seems to love her, though she does most of the work in that relationship as far as I can see. I hope he knows what a gem she is."

"How's your new book coming? Or should I not ask? Last time you said it was slow going."

"Some halting progress. Distractions. There has been another new wrinkle in my life of late."

"You going to make me guess?"

"A *man*." Marian drew out the word.

"Really? That's great Marian."

"We've had a few…get togethers. He's nice."

"Get togethers? Is that what they're calling *dates* here in New York these days?"

"Very funny."

"So, tell me about this man of mystery."

"His name is Charles. Used to import wine from France. Widower. Pretty recent."

"How did you meet this wine importer?"

"Well, it's sort of a little odd."

"I'm okay with odd. At our age, odd works. There is no *normal*."

"Our spouses are buried in the same cemetery, so we sort of ran into each other."

"You had *dates* there?"

"No!"

"Okay. I feel better. There's odd and then there's macabre."

"We meet at a tea shop."

"How many times have you...*met* him?"

"Three or four now."

"Nothing in the evening yet?"

"No. Not yet."

"Do you want to?"

"If he suggests it."

"Are you attracted to him?"

"He's actually quite good looking."

"So that's a yes?"

"You know I'm not good at talking about this stuff." She paused and sipped her drink. "Yes. I find him attractive. Lord knows why he wants to look at me."

"Don't be silly."

"I have lines on my face that could hide a small child." Marian laughed and Hilary almost choked on her coffee.

"You're a famous poet for god sakes, and Nathan was not an unattractive man, as I recall."

"Please don't tell me you slept with him, too," Marian said playfully.

"Not that I remember, and I think I would've, especially given the fact that I was a virgin all the way through college."

"Probably better off. Do you want more? It's decaf."

Hilary nodded and Marian walked into the kitchen.

"Do you really have to leave in the morning?" Marian said while picking up the pot.

"Roland has never been to New York City."

"Never? You really did find yourself a man off the beaten path."

"Yeah, he's definitely a West Coast guy. I promised I would take him around the city, and we booked a suite in a romantic hotel by the park."

"Okay. I can't compete with Central Park."

"So, are you really going to give this man a chance? Are you ready?"

"I didn't think so, to be honest. Now, I'm not sure."

"I think you should stay with it as long as you feel good about it."

Marian nodded and took a sip of her coffee. It was a funny thing about company, she mused. When she didn't have any for long stretches, she didn't feel lonely. But when she had good company, she remembered what she missed about it. In the morning, when Hilary and Roland left for the City, the house would be tranquil, unnaturally quiet, and she would be alone again with the ghosts. The anticipation was unnerving. The ghosts would sometimes sit with her as she silently made breakfast or dinner and she would hear them argue or laugh depending on her mood. Mira as a child was the most vocal. Who could forget that giggle?

25

village

1985

The only thing standing in the breach between Nathan and total despair was Martin. After almost three months in Queens away from Marian and his little girl, he was close to losing all hope. But every time he was ready to surrender to his hopelessness and leave New York altogether, Martin would abandon his usual sarcasm and earnestly convince him leaving was not a viable option. Martin cautioned once he closed the door on New York, he would make it easy for Marian to dismiss him and his "wandering dick". As Martin noted, she hadn't called to say she wanted a divorce, and was still sending his mail in a manila envelope once a week. She had even picked up the phone about a month after he left to tell him to stop calling because she was afraid he would upset Mira. In other words, not because she wanted to hang his cheating ass from the highest tree in the City. There were glimmers of hope and between glasses of red wine, Martin and his steady stream of acolytes were convinced she would eventually take him back. On probation, of course. He wasn't so sure but their optimism kept him sane while he rode the subway night after night across the East River back to his personal prison in Queens.

Martin had somehow persuaded Nathan to head with him to the Village this particular night and join him at his favorite haunt. He had never been to a gay bar, but he thought it might be interesting. He reasoned it was probably a good thing that there were no temptations. He assumed he would just be hanging out with the same entertaining and eclectic crowd that populated Martin's living room several nights a week. He hadn't anticipated they would start to separate within minutes of arriving. Martin and his friends clearly were not interested in sitting around a table knocking back beers.

So, Nathan decided to sit at the bar and watch as Martin used his considerable charm on new *acquaintances,* as he liked to call them. The only complication was the other men in the bar assumed Nathan was available. By the time he took a swig of his first beer, a man about twice his age with close cropped gray hair and a tattoo on his forearm starting chatting with him. Nathan hadn't considered that he might have to spend the evening fending off men.

"I'd buy you a beer, but you already have one."

He smiled and Nathan could see he was a missing a tooth on the right side of his mouth. Nathan thought he wouldn't be interested, even if he was gay.

"Yeah, I'm good. Thanks."

"I've never seen you here. New to the neighborhood?"

"I live on the Upper West Side."

"Nice. I grew up in Hell's Kitchen. Not far, but a million miles away, if you know what I mean."

Although he recognized the name, Nathan couldn't remember where Hell's Kitchen was.

"I hear you."

"What do you do?"

"I teach sixth grade. History."

"In the City?"

"Not too far from here. Lower East Side."

"Nice. You here alone or with friends?"

"Oh. Yeah. I came with some friends. I didn't mean to be rude."

"You weren't rude. I meant, are you looking for someone?"

Nathan didn't understand for a few seconds and then read something else on his face.

"Oh. No. I'm not gay."

"You're in a gay bar. You know that, right?"

"I came with friends."

"That's too bad. You're very cute and those dimples are killing me."

"I'm flattered. That's probably the nicest thing anyone has said to me in months."

"Are you fucking with me?"

"No. I'm not. My wife kicked me out a few months ago."

"That sucks. You fuck around on her?"

"Do I look like I would fuck around?"

"I could see women coming on to you. I just put two and two together."

"Have you cheated on someone?"
"You don't want to ask me."
"Why not?"
"I was married to a woman a long time ago and I was fucking lots of men. That didn't end well."
"Yeah, but that's different."
"Is it? I don't know. If you ask my ex, she'd probably say she had a lot in common with your wife."

Nathan nodded and waved the bartender over and ordered two beers and two shots for him and his new friend. The man thanked him and said: "To cheating men."

Nathan clinked glasses with him and downed his first shot. Before too long Nathan was drunk and a few hours later he walked out of the bar and waved a taxi down. At some point during the last hour he had convinced himself that he was going to see Marian tonight and plead his case. He visualized her sleeping in their bed, probably next to Mira. He belonged there and not in some apartment in Queens. As much as he liked Martin, he was an interloper and wasn't supposed to be there. He barely noticed where they were until the taxi stopped in front of their brownstone. He fished out some money, paid the cabbie, and spilled out onto the quiet street. He hadn't brought his key, so he had no choice but to ring the bell, which was sure to wake Mira. He waited and there was no response. He rang it again and still no response. He stepped back into the street to see if the apartment was still dark. No lights. He decided to ring it one more time and, this time, the door buzzed, and he was so surprised that he almost forgot to push it open before the sound stopped. Marian appeared in a nightshirt and shielded her eyes from the street light.

"Hey." Nathan wanted to grab her.
"You're drunk."
"A little." Nathan said sheepishly.
"Where have you been?"
"Queens."
"I meant tonight."
"Oh. A gay bar in the Village with Martin."
"That's new."
"I'm lost. I want to come home."
"Look, come inside. You're going to wake everyone up out here."

Nathan followed Marian to the living room and sat on the couch. He could feel himself fading, but he was *in*. A few second later his eyes shut and Marian could see him falling asleep. He *did* look lost. Did three months in the wilderness teach him a lesson? She had to admit she missed him too and Mira had no father. Mira wore her baseball cap to sleep most nights, hoping that it would bring home Nathan from his now very lengthy "work" trip. Luckily, children had no sense of time. When he started snoring, she went and got him a blanket. There wouldn't be any conversation tonight. Once she let him in the house, she knew there was probably no turning back, especially after Mira woke up. She sat across from him and watched him sleep soundly. He was going to have a monster hangover, that was for sure. She knew she had let him in the door for a reason. Instinct? She hoped it was a sound one.

26

party

Marian wasn't sure if she was awake or dreaming. It seemed like she was in a familiar looking hotel room in Spain. There was a wooden carving of the crucifixion above the dresser and she heard the waves lapping against the shore outside the window. She got out of bed to look in the mirror and she saw herself as young again. She could see someone stirring in the bed behind her and turned around. The man rolled over. A shirtless Charles lifted his head and smiled at her. She covered her breasts. The phone rang and she startled. Her hands were still covering her chest, but she was wearing a nightgown. She remembered something about Spain and heard Charles's voice on her answering machine. He was saying something about his daughter, but she was too far away to make out what he was saying. She looked at the clock and counted about five hours of sleep. She had been up late trying to finish the opening stanza of a poem about the night after she buried Nathan:

146   THE WIDOW *Verses*

> *There were tiny pieces of me*
> *floating here and there*
> *having broken off*
> *in the middle of the night*

Marian got up and went into the bathroom and looked in the mirror. Her hair was hanging down in her face, and it occurred to her that she really needed a haircut. She picked up a brush from the vanity and tried to brush out the knots to no avail. She walked to the kitchen, saw the blinking message and hit the button. Charles wanted her to come to his daughter's son's first birthday party. Even though she anticipated the possibility because Charles had been talking about his grandson's upcoming party, the idea of meeting a room full of strangers was daunting, even if she was mildly curious to meet his family. It hadn't even been a year since his wife had passed. What would they think of her? She could feel the chilly reaction already. She would have to tell him it wasn't an idea she was comfortable with. In the daughter's house, there would be pictures on a piano or hanging on a long hallway wall arranged just so, and Charles could be standing there next to his lovely French bride. She would see the story that wasn't supposed to ever end, until it did. What would she be? A tacked on ending that didn't fit with the rest of the story and wasn't supposed to be written? She replayed the message looking for clues as to whether he really expected her to agree. It wasn't a hard sell, but he did say that his daughter would be "happy to meet you if you were inclined to come." She hadn't realized he told anyone about their dating. They had only been seeing each other for four months. After showering, she decided to call Hilary. She hadn't spoken to her since she left New York. She would surely have an opinion about this party.

"Marian? I was thinking about you yesterday. You must have heard me."

"Poet's sixth sense? How did the rest of your trip go?"

"New York in the fall. What's not to like? The park was so pretty. So many colors. We don't get that here. It made me nostalgic. I'm an East Coast gal in my bones."

"Roland like it?"

"Oh, I think he was pretty overwhelmed. Not a big city guy. I think there were way too many people for him."

"Seems like a nice man."

"Thanks. He is. So far, so good."

"So, speaking of so far so good, I have a dilemma."

"Sounds intriguing."

"I was invited to Charles's grandson's first birthday party. As his date."

"No grass growing under his feet."

"That's the problem. I sort of like when the grass grows. I don't know if this is a good idea."

"Too fast?"

"We've only been together for about four months."

"Well, he's clearly comfortable enough in your relationship to invite you to meet his family. Even when we were much younger, that's a pretty big step. A signal to his family."

"I get that and that's nice."

"Can I be frank?"

"That's why I called. I need your perspective."

"I know you're a good Midwestern girl at heart, and I know your parents raised you right, but it's not like opportunities are growing on trees for widowed sixty-five-year-old poets living in the burbs, you know what I mean?"

"Ouch. You really meant it."

"I just don't want you to miss out on something that might be good because of some timeline in your head. In the big picture, it's just a house party, and most of the guests will be focusing on the little boy, not you. There is no need to build this up like you're Cinderella going to the ball. You can easily retreat to the background. Don't talk yourself out of going for all sorts of reasons. If you like spending time with Charles, join him at the party."

"What happened to shy, retiring Hilary?"

"She got tired of life passing her by." Hilary laughed.

～

Why did Hilary have to mention Cinderella? She couldn't get the image out of her mind. Charles looked even more distinguished than usual and she kept imagining he was the prince as he drove to his daughter's home.

"You're pretty quiet."

"Sorry. Are you sure she's okay with this? I know you said she was, but what if she didn't mean it? I would certainly understand."

"Kristin is a big girl. She understands that life has to march forward."

Charles put his hand on hers and looked at her. She put her other hand on his. The clamminess was hers.

"By the way, Kristin's husband is Lucas. He's a nice young man. Not crazy about his parents, who are divorced."

"What does Lucas do?"

"Something in finance. Bonds maybe? They met in business school."

"Sounds like they share a love of money."

"She was our practical child. My son was the dreamer."

They pulled into the driveway, and Charles reached for her hand as they walked into the door. Marian felt like dragging Charles back to the car. Hugs and quick kisses were the extent of their intimacy to this point since they were typically meeting and leaving separately. To her, holding hands was a more intimate gesture. Marian immediately recognized Kristin, with her long curly black hair and piercing blue eyes, from the cemetery. She thought about taking her hand away from Charles, but she decided that there was no turning back and she needed to show a united front.

"Hi. I'm Kristin."

"Kristin, so nice to meet you. Congratulations."

"Thank you. So, my father says you're a famous writer."

"I don't know about famous. I've published some collections."

"Well, my father is impressed, and it takes a lot to impress him, so you must be quite accomplished."

"That's kind of you to say."

"My mother used to paint. She was really quite good, though we couldn't ever convince her to show her work to anyone but family and close friends."

"Well, I wish there were some crossover between writing and art but, unfortunately, I can't draw at all. I'd like to see her paintings one day."

Marian didn't know why she had made that last remark. She thought it might have been too intrusive. Kristin just nodded and said she had to greet her aunt who had just walked in. Marian said she understood and thanked her for allowing her to come.

"You didn't tell me Nathalie painted."

"She *was* quite good. Her paintings are all over the house."

"I'm not sure I could handle that."

"Handle that?"

"If I were you, I mean. I have some photos of Nathan in a few places but having her essence all around me…."

"I guess I never thought of it that way."

Charles saw his son Henry and waved him over. Henry didn't look like Charles at all, and Marian surmised she was looking at a version of his late wife.

"I wanted you to meet Marian. This is Henry."

"Nice to meet you, Henry."

"Hello." Henry said without much enthusiasm. Or, maybe it was a whiff of caution. Marian couldn't tell.

"Charles tells me you are a natural at running the wine business." Marian didn't like fibbing but she wasn't sure what else to say and felt she had already blown the Kristin introduction.

"I don't know about that."

Charles could see that Henry was fidgety.

"There's a lot of *family* here so I can't spread myself too thin. Lots of people to say hello to."

Marian looked at Charles and they were thinking the same thing. Maybe her presence was too much for him.

"Okay Henry. We'll talk later."

"Nice to meet you, Marian."

"Likewise."

Henry walked away and Charles waited until he was far enough away to speak.

"I'm sorry."

"About what? It's understandable."

"Maybe. He is really a nice boy."

"I'm sure he is."

"Funny thing is, he is the one urging me to live my life."

"Well, it's one thing to tell you that, and it's another to see another woman who isn't your mother standing next to your father."

Throughout the rest of the afternoon Marian's thoughts drifted between Henry's reaction to her and Charles' house. She wondered what Nathalie painted and why she painted them. Also, she wondered if Henry wasn't right. Who was she to step into his mother's shoes? At the end of the evening, Kristin thanked everyone for coming and then spoke about the person missing from the room. At one point, teary-eyed she glanced at her father biting his lower lip. Since the first time she had seen him at the cemetery, this was the only time she had seen him anything less than cheerful. Marian dropped her hand to his knee. He looked over at her and forced a smile.

"Thank you for inviting me."

"You're a good sport."

"Charles."

"I don't know you that well, but I'm smart enough to figure out that maybe I rushed this."

Introspection. A trait, she observed, not inherent to Nathan.

"Maybe a little." Marian made her *it's not so bad* face. Nathan always said it was cute and would kiss her during those moments.

"I apologize. Can you forgive me?"

"There's nothing to apologize for or to forgive. You have a lovely family."

"Thank you. I just thought…"

"It was a nice thought and I'm still flattered you wanted them to meet me."

He patted her hand and they got up to say their goodbyes. Marian waited in the doorway while Charles retrieved her coat. There was a long oak table below a silver-framed mirror crowded with family pictures. Ten-year-old Henry stared at her holding a fish nearly half his size. Charles stood to the side beaming. He was so tan she almost didn't recognize him. Her eyes scanned the other pictures and she came upon a recent picture of Kristin, clearly quite pregnant, standing next to her smiling cancer-ravaged mother, who was wearing a stylish wool cap to cover up her bald head. Kristin was playfully holding her mother by the head and leaning in so that their faces were touching. Marian was about to cry but quickly turned from the photos when Henry appeared out of nowhere.

"I'm sorry about before."

"No worries. Really."

Marian was sure Henry could see her tears and looked away toward the picture of his mother with Kristin.

"She was something. If I could be half as content as her someday, I'd be a lucky guy. She took everything in stride. Even her cancer. Or at least that's what it seemed."

"Well, sounds like you are already a lucky guy. Having her as a mother I mean."

Henry nodded in agreement and Charles came down the stairs with her coat. Marian put her hand on Henry's shoulder and said goodnight. In the driveway, Charles turned to her.

"What was that about?"

"He's still grieving in his own way. I think he wanted me to know."

"I guess I'm not the greatest at drawing that out from my children."

"I think my daughter might say the same of me. Sometimes it's easier or makes more sense to let people, even family, cope with their own pain. Once you start asking questions you might have to examine your own grief."

On the way home the front seat seemed more crowded with ghosts than on the way there. When they arrived at her house, in Marian's imagination, Nathan opened the car door and trailed her up the driveway, bemoaning he was still hungry. He never liked party food. Nathalie's specter drifted closer to Charles. He could smell her scent, which made him smile. Charles waved goodbye to Marian and he thought he heard Natalie say she's good for you.

27

garden

1986

*M*arian had been thinking about leaving the city for a while. The apartment was becoming claustrophobic with Mira and her things strewn about. But her "break" from Nathan convinced her they needed a fresh start somewhere else. Their tiny bedroom would always hold the memory of the night she confronted Nathan, and she needed to distance herself from it. She and Mira trailed Nathan with the agent as they walked. This particular house held little interest for Marian. In each place, they visited, she tried to imagine herself writing. Would the house and the environs provide any degree of inspiration? As with many others they visited, this particular house was distinctive only in its utter lack of personality. Marian vowed not to spend years in a cookie cutter house some developer had reconstituted over and over again, block after block.

She knew agents were supposed to be friendly, but she didn't have to laugh at Nathan's every utterance. He was charming, but he wasn't Robert Redford. The agent tossed back her mane of perfect curly long hair every time she laughed. Was it this agent in particular or was she going to react to any woman Nathan talked to now? Marian tried to be rational about it. She thought about telling Nathan she wanted to leave or that they needed to get a new agent. But she decided not to give in to her insecurities, even though the agent touched his elbow while making a point about the kitchen.

Luckily, for Nathan, Mira chose that moment to distract her by asking to use the bathroom. The agent overheard Mira and directed them to a bathroom on the upper floor in the hallway. In the bathroom Mira hopped up on the seat and interrupted Marian's thinking.

"Is this our new house?"
"No, honey."
"Well, where is it?"
"We haven't found it yet."
"Do you know where it is?"
"We're looking."
"Okay. I'm hungry."

Marian turned on the sparkling clean faucet and helped Mira wash her hands as they counted to 15 together. She could see that Mira's nails still stubbornly held the remnants of the purple polish they applied the previous week. Marian fished around in the backpack and pulled out a bag of pretzels and gave them to Mira. They went back downstairs and Marian could hear the agent laughing. She found them in a charmless family room. Marian interrupted.

"Nathan, I don't think this house will work for us." She turned toward the agent. *What was her name?* "Do you have anything else to show us today?" Marian asked sternly.

The agent was flustered for a moment and looked toward Nathan who offered no resistance.

"Oh. Okay. I have another house, not as nice, but with a lot of *character*. Only three bedrooms though." Marian wondered why the agent thought 'only three bedrooms' could possibly be unattractive to a family with a single child.

"There are only three of us. That's fine."

"Right. Okay. Let's take a look."

Nathan caught up to Marian and scooped up Mira, who began flicking his ear. He wondered why she thought earlobes were a toy.

"You really didn't like this place, huh?" Nathan whispered.

"No. And I'm not crazy about this agent. She's showing the houses she wants us, for her reasons, to see, not ones that would appeal to us."

"Seems nice enough."

"A little *too* nice."

Nathan wasn't going to disagree with Marian. He had been sidestepping all conflict since being allowed to return, and he certainly wasn't going to contradict her on this particular issue even if he saw it differently. He sensed Marian's tension, but really didn't know if the agent or the prospect of uprooting was the source. At this point, Nathan concluded that it didn't matter.

"I can see that."

"You can? If you did, you wouldn't have been flirting with her."

"I wasn't trying to. Maybe you should talk with her. You seem to have a more specific idea of what we want anyhow."

Marian buckled Mira into the car seat and then buckled herself in. The *we* wasn't lost on her. She knew he was just placating her, but she also understood that her barely hidden anger was driving his behavior. She just couldn't help it right now. The wound hadn't closed up yet.

"Daddy?"

"Yes, Mira?"

"Mommy needs a hug."

"She does?"

"Yes."

"Okay, honey when I stop driving."

Nathan looked at Marian for some signal as to how to respond. Marian had not initiated any physical contact with him since he returned home. She stared out the windshield as if she hadn't heard Mira's request.

"Daddy is driving right now honey. He can't hug mommy."

"Okay."

They drove in silence to their next destination, which turned out to be a charming house that looked as if the owners had an aversion to paint and nails. Nathan kept a respectful distance as the agent talked of "good bones" and "a lovely piece of property". He just nodded his head politely and waited for a verdict from his newly unpredictable wife. Marian knew this was exactly the sort of house Nathan wasn't interested in, but she could see the possibilities and the backyard seemed to stretch on forever. It reminded her of the house she grew up in, except it didn't have a back porch or deck. The back steps just walked down to the lawn, though that could be remedied. She could see planting a garden in the back and watching Mira run around when she wasn't trying to write. Also, she loved that you couldn't even see the next house in the back because the trees were so thick at the end of the lawn.

"I want it." She whispered to Nathan.

"Yeah?"

"It's a bit...old."

"We can fix it up. You'll see."

Nathan was not interested in house projects, but his desire to make peace with Marian outstripped any aversion to painting walls. He looked around like he was reconsidering. Mira was running around a hulking oak tree in the backyard.

"I think you may be right. This place does have lots of character."

"You just saying that?"

"No. I mean it's going to be some work but, look at her, she can run around and the price is very reasonable."

"So we're making an offer?"

"Sure, let's do it."

When the agent returned from inside, Marian surprised her by telling her that they were interested in making an offer. The agent quickly pivoted and they all began discussing numbers. Marian drifted off to look around more and try and picture them in the house while Nathan continued discussing the pros and cons of various offers with the agent. Marian was already planning that English garden right below the deck they were going to build. She would pick flowers with Mira to populate her kitchen table. She could already envision the scent and warmth they would bring to the house. This was a good place to heal.

28

footprints

The snowstorm that had left most of New England without power was ominously speeding its way to New York. The sky was darkening to a heavy gray and Mira could see that the window sill was starting to get covered. She knew it was only a matter of time before the text messages from Matt would start pinging her phone. He had wanted to leave already, but she insisted on stopping by her mother's house. She told him she needed to make sure there was nothing in her old room she wanted to bring to Seattle. She knew there really wasn't anything she needed, but she wanted to say goodbye to her mother. Her mother had been surprised to see her when she opened the door. Mira made some excuse about forgetting something in her room. For the most part, her room preserved a little girl's ambience.

They had moved in when she was only four, and she had been gone, more or less, since she had left for college. Softball trophies and high school team pictures still lined her bookcase. Soon after they moved in, her father had brought Mira into the backyard and taught her how to catch and throw a baseball. No one at school could understand why she wasn't a Yankees fan given their proximity to the Bronx, or how she had the nerve to wear a Cardinals hat. In school, she considered it a badge of courage. Her allegiance only grew and calcified when she was taunted by the boys. Father and daughter against the Yankee empire. Fortuitously, the Yankees were in decline during a substantial portion of her childhood, so her classmates had very little to crow about.

At some point, she knew her mother would sell her precious house and its impeccable garden. How many more times would she get to sit in her old room or see the backyard which held so many memories? Seattle was a long way from New York, and she didn't expect to be coming home every few months. She was lost in thought and didn't notice her mother had crept into the room.

"Don't you think you should go? It's getting nasty out there."

"I should."

"Are you taking anything?"

"Oh. Yeah. I was going to take a few of my high school yearbooks."

Marian picked up one of her trophies and read the inscription.

"Your dad loved to watch you play. He would give me a play by play analysis of your games. You were always the focal point."

"I always assumed he wanted a boy."

"A boy? Never heard him say that. He enjoyed every moment of your sports career."

"I don't know. I just assumed given his love of baseball. Girls don't play baseball."

"One day you'll understand that disappointment is impossible when you find out or the doctors tell you the sex of your child. In that moment, the connection is so powerful, you could be told you are having a baby chick and you might spontaneously start clucking and flapping your arms."

They both laughed and when they stopped, Marian could see that leaving was weighing on Mira. Over the past few weeks, she had been thinking about how much she would miss her little girl who was in truth, a grown woman. Since the original conversation when Mira told her she was moving to Seattle, she hadn't really considered how Mira might feel.

"You know I'm going to be okay?" Miriam offered.

"I know."

"We can talk as much as you like. I'll even text if that makes you happy."

"Wow. I must really look sad." Mira tried to smile.

"A little. I already promised Hilary I'm visiting her in California in the spring. Seattle can't be that far."

"That's good. I didn't expect to be so nostalgic. But with dad gone."

"Like I said, I'll be fine. So, will you. I have a *boyfriend* you know." Marian tried to proclaim it as if she was a 16-year-old high school girl.

"That's another thing. I barely got to know Charles. I feel bad about that. I should have made more of an effort."

"Well, if he doesn't get tired of me soon, maybe I'll haul him out to Seattle."

"That would be cool. He seems nice. Different than dad. But nice."

"Unfortunately, there isn't a clone catalogue where you

can check off boxes and create similar life forms. Of course, we would want to change a few strands of DNA."

"He wasn't perfect."

"Oh, not by a country mile, but you don't need to listen to an old wife blather."

"I know he cheated on you mom."

Marian's legs felt a little wobbly and she thought she might topple over. She wasn't expecting *that*. How do you talk to your daughter about something like that?

"I don't even want to know how you know. It's not important. I didn't want you to have to worry about all that."

"I overheard Uncle Gordon talking to dad about it."

"I'm sorry you found out."

Marian wondered if Nathan was aware that Mira had heard him. If he was, then he never shared it with her. More secrets.

"You have nothing to be sorry about it. I just hope you didn't stay with him because of me."

"No. I just had to get my head out of the clouds. I wanted poetry, and sometimes I got heartache. I had to come to terms with what I valued, and whether that was possible anymore. In the end, I took another chance on your father."

"Were you happy you did?"

Marian paused again. It was a question she avoided asking herself for years. She plowed ahead living her life and crossed her fingers that she wouldn't find some residue of an affair or a one-night stand on Nathan's clothes. She never quite got used to him speaking with other women, especially if she thought they were pretty. She didn't want her daughter thinking of her as an object of pity. A woman who remained in some loveless marriage. She also didn't want her daughter spending time dwelling on her father's foibles. She had to wonder if Mira picked up on something in how they talked or related to each other. She was so small when their break had occurred, she always figured Mira would be unaffected or would barely understand or remember. Did Mira pick up on her anger? In the end she decided to be pithy.

"Yes."

"That's it? Yes?"

"What do you want me to say? You want me to recount the ups and downs of my marriage? You're a woman now, Mira. Is any relationship between two people perfect?"

"No. But I had boyfriends who cheated on me and I dumped them."

Marian realized how little she actually knew about her daughter's emotional life. However, she was happy to hear she stood up for herself.

"It's a little more complicated when you're married with a child."

"I get that. I do. I'm not trying to upset you. I'm just trying to understand."

"As I said before, I made a choice. Your father was the great love of my life. I didn't want to lose that."

"I hope you're telling me the truth. He's not here now, so there's no reason not to."

Except you're my daughter, Marian thought. There are some things that shouldn't pass between us.

"It's getting bad out there honey. You really should go."

Mira nodded and Marian followed Mira down the stairs. She wanted to reach out and stroke her hair one last time, but she wasn't a little girl anymore. Their conversation was certainly proof of that. Mira got to the door, turned around and hugged her mother. Mira said goodbye, and Marian watched her walk to her car. Enough snow had fallen already so that her footprints were visible. By the time she drove away, her footprints had already begun to fade as the snow fell harder. Seattle seemed a million miles away. How was she going to protect her all the way out there? She hoped Mira didn't think she was pathetic. What if she knew it was the second time Nathan had cheated on her? Marian didn't want to think about it anymore. She went back inside to make a pot of tea.

29

grand rapids

1988

*M*arian couldn't recall the last time she had seen the Grand River. When she was a child, she was fascinated by how it seemed to cut through Grand Rapids, as if it had barged in between the buildings and asserted its right-of-way. Seeing the river again, made her sort of melancholy to think about how pristine it might have looked a century ago, before most of the buildings stood up along its banks. In Manhattan it was nearly impossible to imagine the island bereft of the mighty skyscrapers, but here you could close your eyes and brush the buildings away. Since Nathan's parents had been weathering one health crisis after another the past few years, they had been foregoing their usual trips to Michigan. Her mother said she understood, and she did have her companion Christopher now. Nonetheless, Marian still felt guilty that it had been so long.

As they turned onto her street, Marian she could see her mother sitting on the front porch slowly rocking in her favorite chair. She used to peer out the windows of the school bus to catch a glimpse of her when she was a child. During the warmer months, her mother would sit and knit or read a book at some point during the day. It wasn't until she focused on the property that she noticed that there was a sign from a realtor on the front lawn. Her stomach dropped when she saw the sign. When they stopped, Mira bounded out of the car and up the steps. As she got closer to the lawn, she recognized the realtor's photo on the sign as a girl she grew up with. The realtor boasted a ridiculous haircut so unwieldy that it nearly swallowed the photo.

"I can't believe how tall she is now Marian."

"Seven going on eight."

"I know. I see Nathan never ages."

"Oh, I wish it were so, Janet." Nathan waited for Mira to finish hugging her grandmother and then gave her a peck on the cheek. Marian stood on the porch and surveyed the neighborhood for signs of change. The Robertson's house looked refreshed with coffee colored siding and a basketball hoop dominating the driveway. She couldn't imagine the aging couple shooting baskets.

"The Robertsons?"

"Gone. They sold the house and moved into one of those over fifty-five communities last year. Nice young family moved in."

"The sign?"

"I wanted to tell you about that."

"Really?"

"I thought it would be better in person."

"Okay. I'm waiting."

"A developer offered me a lot of money. He wants to combine our property and the Mattison's."

Marian couldn't believe her mother would sell to a developer. She loved the house and property as much as Marian did.

"And Christopher says the offer is above market value," her mother said.

"Oh, he does? Is he a real estate expert? I thought he sold plastics or something."

"You're being hysterical. It's not like you're moving back."

"Maybe I would." She looked over at Nathan who knew she was being less than honest.

"No, you're not."

"Well, now it's not an option. Let's step back a second. If a developer had offered you gobs of money out of the clear blue, then there wouldn't be a sign with all that girl's hair in the yard."

"Girl's hair?"

"You know what I'm talking about. Ginnie or whatever her name is."

"Winnie. And she is a very sweet girl. Well, Christopher thought it would be a good idea to see what we could get with the market so high right now"

"Christopher. Do you do whatever he says now?"

Marian knew she shouldn't have said that, but it was too late to take it back now. Her mother just stood there looking hurt. Nathan looked at her and waited for her to say something to at least try and diffuse the standoff. When she didn't, he stepped in.

"I'm sure your mom is doing what she thought was best for her. She can't live in this big house forever."

"Nathan's right. It's too much for me now. I can't believe I forgot to take the sign in before you got here, but I never thought you'd be so upset."

Marian couldn't even identify with certainty what made her so upset, but she couldn't seem to slow her mounting anger.

"I wanted to wait until Christopher got back from the store, but I might as well tell you now and get it over with."

"What now? You're running away with the circus?"

"You are very fresh today Marian Elizabeth. Christopher and I are getting married."

"When?" was all Marian could think to say. She actually liked Christopher so she tried to control herself.

"Well, Christopher had this crazy idea that we do it Sunday, as long as you're all here."

Nathan noticed Mira had been observing the battle being waged by her mother and grandmother with little discernible comprehension, but as soon as a wedding was mentioned she perked up.

"Married?" Mira squealed.

"Yes, honey."

"A wedding? Am I in it? Can I be in it, grandma?"

"Of course. You can be our flower girl."

"Cool. Is that okay, mom?"

"Wow. We didn't pack for a wedding," Nathan said and shook his head. His comment drove Marian careening in yet another direction.

"Yeah, wow. Why did you wait to tell me now?"

"Of course, I was planning on telling you, but Christopher brought this up last week, and at first I thought it was crazy. Then I thought, I'm not interested in some lavish wedding, and so why not? Everyone I love will be here, right?"

Marian was stopped cold by the last sentence. Her mother didn't throw *that* word around very often. Her mother seemed happy, and who was she to rain on her parade? She was trying to envision her mother in a white wedding dress, but couldn't wrap her head around it. And Nathan was right. What in the world would all of them wear?

"I can't argue with that." Marian decided to lay down her arms for now.

"Good. Christopher and I want to take all of you on a shopping excursion this afternoon so we can buy you some new clothes."

"Fun." Mira exclaimed.

At the mall, Mira was flitting in and out of the stores with Janet. Marian never really liked to shop, so she was glad her mother was helping Mira. Bored, Marian kept thinking she was bound to run into someone from high school, but she didn't recognize anyone. The lack of familiar faces as they strolled among the throngs reminded her how long she had been away. Christopher conspicuously stayed back and walked with her most of the time. He clearly wanted to talk.

"I hope you're not mad at your mother for holding back. I think the surprise was less important than not wanting to answer questions until you arrived. In fact, if it wasn't for a recent diagnosis of mine, she might not have agreed."

"What diagnosis?"

"I wasn't sure if she was going to tell you herself. I have a blood cancer. They're treating it, and hopefully I won't be going anywhere for a while." Christopher smiled and Marian noticed that he was thinner than usual. He was always lanky with a rather thin longish face, so she hadn't picked up on his weight loss.

"I wish she would've told me. How long have they been treating you?"

"I guess about six months. I don't think she wanted to worry you. You know how she is."

"I do. If there is anything I can do to help, please ask. They have great doctors and hospitals in New York."

"Thank you. I think I found a good oncologist."

"I'm very glad to hear that."

"I've been asking her to marry me for a long time."

"Really?" Marian wasn't actually surprised.

"She was always worried about your reaction, I think."

"My reaction? She doesn't typically share much with me."

"You're a towering figure in that house." Christopher smiled so she wouldn't take offense.

"I am?"

"Well, she tells anyone and everyone about her daughter the famous poet. And, I think she might feel guilty about the way your father treated you."

"My father?"

"He wasn't the most affectionate fellow, from what I hear."

"Oh. *That*."

Marian had never really given much thought to what her mother shared with Christopher. They had been together for years, so Marian surmised that perhaps her mother had opened up. Marian didn't really want to discuss her father with Christopher, even if he wasn't mistaken. It felt like a betrayal of sorts. Christopher could sense she was getting uncomfortable.

"I didn't mean to upset you. I was just trying to explain. The important thing is she said yes, and she desperately wants your approval."

"I told her years ago I was fine with it. She doesn't need my approval."

All of a sudden it occurred to Marian that her mother had waited all this time to marry him so that *she* would be comfortable with it. Her mother had wanted to marry him all those years ago when they were in Detroit together on her book tour. Maybe her mother didn't think she was ready?

"But she does. I guess children don't always understand their power. Parents are loathe to do anything to make their children unhappy, even if it hurts them."

Marian could see why her mother was so happy now. She always liked Christopher, but she hadn't really tried to get to know him well. He was so different from her father. So much more of an open book.

"Don't worry. I'll talk to her. Sunday will be a great day for all of us."

Marian could see that Christopher was on the verge of tears, and she put her hand on his shoulder.

"Thank you." Christopher said with relief.

∽

Marian assumed Christopher discussed their conversation with her mother, but she knew she still needed to talk with her. Nathan had agreed to be Christopher's best man, so on the way to the church it was just the two of them and Mira in the back seat. Mira was wearing earphones and listening to music.

"So, I spoke with Christopher."

"Yes, he was very happy."

"He's a nice man."

"I'm glad you think so. I don't think he thought you liked him."

"That's not true. I was sad to hear about his cancer. Why didn't you tell me?"

"I don't know. He's been doing so well with the treatments. Maybe I was hoping it would just go away."

"Like with dad?"

"No, that was different. I knew there wasn't much hope. I tried to stay positive for you."

"I'm thirty-seven now, mother. I can handle these things."

"I know. I'm sorry."

"How is he doing now?"

"Pretty well, I think. It's in remission."

"Good. By the way, you look very pretty."

"I do?"

"Like a blushing bride."

Marian took her eyes off the road and grinned.

"I would have been fine with a justice of the peace. Christopher insisted on a church ceremony."

"I'm glad he did. You deserve a day in the sun."

"Thank you. You're going to make me cry."

"You know I would've been fine with you marrying him a long time ago. I told you that in Detroit."

"I know, but I was afraid you were just saying that to make me happy."

"You know me pretty well mother. I'm not very good at shading the truth."

"It's okay. I didn't mind living by myself. For a long time, I didn't think I would, or even that I could."

"You've always been stronger than you thought."

"Maybe. How are things with Nathan?"

"We're good. *She* adores him." Marian motioned to the back seat. Mira was now singing along with the music.

"I can see that. Daughters love their fathers no matter what." Marian didn't reply. She just nodded. She knew her mother was aware that Nathan had done something appalling three years ago to get him kicked out of the apartment. They had never discussed the specifics, and she wasn't interested in her advice then or a post-mortem now. Marian pulled up in front of the church. Nathan was standing in front wearing a rented tuxedo. When he saw Marian, he broke into a wide smile. Mira got out of the car and ran to him. He opened his arms, and she buried herself in his embrace. Marian trailed behind with her mother, making sure she didn't trip. Nathan pulled her up the last step.

"The Collingswood women can really clean up," Nathan teased.

"Thank you, I think."

"Time to get married," Nathan winked.

Nathan and her mother stood at the back of the church and waited for everyone to assemble in their seats. Mira stayed with them so she could fulfill her flower girl duties. Marian settled into the first row after saying hello to Christopher's children, whom she really didn't know. Christopher was chatting with the minister about something. As the organist dove into Here Comes the Bride, Marian looked back to see her mother and Nathan preparing to walk down the aisle. Mira was already walking with a white basket once teeming with flower petals and tossing them on the floor, or sometimes on guests sitting closest to the aisle. She maintained a shy smile on her face and when her eyes connected with Marian she winked, which made Marian chuckle to herself.

Nathan and her mother began to walk slowly together arm in

arm. Marian remembered how Mira used to ask why she wasn't in her parents' wedding pictures. Marian tried to explain she wasn't born yet, but Mira couldn't imagine a family event without her. She probably challenged her own mother with the same question and received a similarly less than satisfactory answer. Yet here she was, at her own mother's wedding. She wondered if her mother was contemplating her first trip down the aisle. Hard to imagine she wouldn't be. When she became an adult, she thought of her mother as spineless for taking whatever her father dished out. It was only in recent years that she wondered if her mother stayed with him to protect her. Christopher shook Nathan's hand with vigor, and Nathan walked over to where they were sitting. She didn't know if they were both lying to her about the extent of his cancer and its prognosis. She considered the possibility this impromptu wedding really served as a final act of love. As the minister spoke, she imagined the angel of death hovering above his head. As if on cue, Mira tugged on her skirt and she looked down and then looked back up again to see her mother kissing Christopher and the angel had disappeared.

30

hiding

$\mathcal{M}$arian stood in the hallway of Charles' house and stared at the painting over the stairs. Charles was still looking for the glasses he wore when they drove and she heard him utter a curse. It was, to her recollection, the first time he had cursed since they had met. A crack in the armor perhaps? She turned back to the painting. How could she tell anyone that she was inspired by the painting of her boyfriend's dead wife? Yet, here she was wanting to make up an excuse and go home to write. But she knew how rude that would be, so she started writing on the imaginary pad she had created in her brain.

look for me
darling
in the colors
in the brushstrokes

> *hiding*
> *amid the blues*
> *behind the golds*

"Marian?"

She didn't notice him standing there.

"Are you okay?"

He was holding his glasses and rubbing his knee with some vigor.

"Are you?" she asked.

"I just whacked my knee on the bedpost."

"I was just…looking. Admiring."

"That's one of my favorites. She painted that when we went to France and stayed in her aunt's farmhouse."

Of course, she did. Marian thought.

"And that was yesterday, right?"

"Day before." Charles grinned.

"You haven't mentioned her recently. I don't mind, you know?"

"I know."

"Has Henry said anything to you lately?"

"No. Kristin mentioned the other day that she'd like to get to know you better."

"That's sweet."

"I think she's been reading about you on the Internet."

"Anything in particular?"

"She wanted to know more about your books."

"You said she doesn't read much."

"Henry was more of the reader."

"You ready to go?"

Charles closed the door behind them. He wanted to tell Marian that most of the time he couldn't bring himself to say Nathalie's name. He was never sure if he could say her name without tearing up. He wasn't sure how Marian would feel if she saw him reduced to a puddle of tears. She might think he wasn't ready to move forward. He wasn't even completely sure himself, but he didn't want to lose her.

~

Nathalie knew it was cruel to leave the children with Charles back at the farm house, but she needed some time away. Kristin just wanted him to acknowledge her, and Henry wanted him to play with him so badly. From time to time, he would show them glimpses of the father they wanted. On occasion, Nathalie would watch as he sat next to Kristin and stroked her hair. The expression on her face said it all. He usually didn't make it home until sundown, and he worked almost every Saturday, so there was little time to throw a ball with Henry. When he made the time, Henry looked like he was going to burst with excitement.

Nathalie was making her way down the path to the lake hauling her easel and paints, but stopped when she heard voices. Through the trees, she could see a young couple quickly taking their clothes off at the water's edge. They couldn't have been more than eighteen. She watched from behind the tree line as they leapt into the water and drew towards one another. She didn't want to interrupt them, so she put her easel down and waited. Before long the image of them embracing and kissing in the lake moved Nathalie to paint furiously in silence. She could see something they were too young to realize and wanted to capture: an exquisite moment in their lives that would never again happen in quite the same way. Whether together or apart, in the future when they are older, they would recall this moment. She also knew before long they would be making love by the lake. She painted as much as she could as they parted and then came together again and again to kiss. She wanted to catch the spontaneity of the scene. When they began to slog their way out of the water, she grabbed up her easel and snuck one last look behind her. She couldn't remember the last time she and Charles experienced a carefree moment that wasn't thought out to some degree.

When she approached the farmhouse, she heard Kristin yelling at Henry and the spell was broken. She drew a deep breath and walked up the hill into the backyard. Charles was nowhere to be found. Nathalie separated the children and went looking for Charles. She found him relaxing in their bedroom. He was listening to music with headphones on sipping a glass of wine. She ripped the headphones off.

"If you understood French better, I would be cursing you out."

"I can't listen to music?"

"No. Not with your kids at each other's throats."

"They can work it out."

"No, they can't."

"I'm sorry."

"No, you're not."

"Why are you back so soon? I thought you wanted to paint."

"The lake was...occupied."

Charles loved how she said certain English words with her French intonation. He knew he was a pretty lousy father, but he never really wanted children. Nathalie wanted them so badly, he didn't have the heart to tell her.

"You want to go into town? That will *occupy* them."

"You're impossible. Alright. Let me wash up. I have paint all over me."

Nathalie went into the bathroom, and Charles saw the canvas she had leaned against the wall on the stone floor. Despite the angle, it appeared to depict two people kissing. He gingerly picked up the painting to inspect it more closely. He understood what Nathalie meant when she said the lake had been occupied. She must have happened upon a couple. He wondered if they really were naked. Given the forms on the canvas, it was hard to tell. Their faces and bodies were painted so close together it looked as if they were almost one person. A single entity. If the children weren't nearby, he could walk into that bathroom right now and make love to her on the floor. He knew if he tried that now she would reject him and tell him they could make love later when the children were asleep. Later, after the children finally went to sleep there would be no moment, no spontaneity. When he met her, he imagined vacations in French farmhouses with her, just like the one they were in now. At the time, those dreams didn't include children who needed to be fed and refereed. He doubted that the couple were thinking about anything other than the clinging dampness of their entwined bodies. With a sigh, Charles gently replaced the canvas and finished the glass of wine. He felt the sway of a slight buzz from the wine. He hoped the accompanying sense of calm might carry him through the afternoon.

31

shea

1996

It was Nathan and Mira's tenth annual pilgrimage to Shea Stadium in Queens to see their beloved Cardinals play the Mets. Intermittently they also mixed in road trips to Pittsburgh, Philadelphia, and Montreal. In recent years, Shea tended to be half full at best. The Mets were experiencing a fallow period in the wake of their 1986 World Series win. The Mets' better players had either scattered to the wind because of age or they had been undermined by external forces. There were some games when rowdy Mets' fans would yell at them for wearing their Cardinals' caps. Usually they were just ignored or sometimes a fan would lament they rooted for the Mets, or wish they were fans of the Cardinals with their far richer history.

Their baseball trips outside of Flushing usually adhered to a certain rhythm. He and Mira would tour areas adjacent to the stadiums and Nathan would eventually come upon kindred spirits and discuss Cardinals lore. Mira understood these were not just daddy and daughter bonding adventures and that Nathan needed to speak with adults. Unfortunately, Shea was not one of those stadiums with anything to offer outside the confines of the stadium. The surrounding area had the feel of a squatter's village with greasy auto body shops having long ago established the gritty character of the neighborhood.

The series was the opener for both teams, and, unlike in 1995, when the baseball season was shortened by a players' strike, the games were beginning in early April. Although the Cardinals had fared poorly in 1995, it was evident that Nathan couldn't wait to get to the ballpark. Mira looked out the car window at the New York City skyline to her far right as he jabbered away about the world being off-kilter since the players had struck in 1994. She was only half listening, because her thoughts kept drifting back to her grandparents' house in Maryland.

On the back porch, her father was arguing with his younger brother Gordon about who was going to care for her grandfather. She was sitting in the kitchen and the door was slightly ajar. She overheard her uncle telling her father he was "congenitally unreliable" and he was surprised Marian hadn't left him a long time ago, especially after he had "fucked around on her." Mira had tried to move but she was frozen. She didn't understand all of the ramifications of what she had just heard, but she knew enough to get that her father had cheated on her mother. They had continued to argue about her grandfather who was lying in bed upstairs, having just returned home from the hospital after a debilitating stroke. Mira wasn't even sure what a stroke was. She thought it had something to do with the brain. All she knew for sure was her once chatty grandfather couldn't speak a word, at least none she could understand. When they walked in to the kitchen, they were both startled to find Mira sitting right there. Nathan had searched her face for any indication she was listening, but she got up and walked away before he could decide.

Mira was so shaken by the argument she wasn't sure what to do with herself, so she walked to the front of the house. Nathan watched as she continued out the front door without a coat. Mira searched for someplace to sit, but March's last snow still partially covered the lawn. Finally, she decided to just lean against the cement columns that held up the front porch. She had desperately wanted to smoke a cigarette, but, since her parents had no clue she smoked, she just imagined inhaling and tried to calm herself.

Her father was still blathering on about some new pitcher the Cardinals had obtained during the offseason. She tried to look interested but she just couldn't muster up the enthusiasm. Since the revelation she tried to look at him the same way, but something was different. She had plenty of friends whose parents were divorced, and she heard rumors about what had broken them apart. But they weren't *her parents,* so they were just stories. She loved her mother, but if someone had asked her two weeks ago whom she would want to live with, she wouldn't have hesitated. Now she wasn't sure if she really knew her father. They liked to make fun of her mother when she was being difficult. He would roll his eyes behind her back sometimes and make her smile. Mira always felt as if they endured her mother's peccadillos together, and now she wondered if it was her mother who was the victim and she was her father's accomplice.

She had, for the most part, avoided him over the past few weeks, but she knew there was no way to beg out of their annual baseball adventure. She wasn't a particularly good actress apparently, so she was afraid something would be written on her face allowing him to read her mind. When it came to her father, she always felt transparent.

"I can't imagine the Grand Central and Queens is that interesting."

"Huh?"

"You've been staring out that window."

"Oh. Just looking."

"Queens has never been my favorite borough."

"It's not really memorable in any particular way."

"No. It's not."

"How's school? You and Chloe still thick as thieves?"

"Thick as?"

"Close. It's an expression."

"Oh. Yeah. We're good."

"You've been a little subdued lately."

"I know, but I'm fine."

"You're almost halfway done."

"School?"

"Yes."

"Everyone says next year is the best."

"Why is that?"

"I guess because you're not a newbie anymore, but you're not getting ready to leave yet."

"That makes sense. Are we going to go on some college road trips next year? We could try to see some games if we're close enough."

"I guess so. That could be fun."

"Could be? A few years ago, you would've killed to see some new ballparks."

"I'm not a little girl anymore."

"I'm a lot older than you. I'm not sure what your age has to do with it."

Mira could tell she hurt his feelings, but for some reason she didn't feel compelled to backtrack. "I don't know what you want me to say."

"Forget about it. I have to focus on the signs anyhow. We're almost there and it's easy to make a wrong turn around here and end up heading in the wrong direction."

Nathan thought they had skated through her early adolescence with a minimum of drama, but it appeared that they had entered some new difficult phase. He turned off at the exit for Shea and followed the flow of traffic. Mira resumed staring out the window, and he wondered if Mira had been humoring him by agreeing to come to the games. She was sporting her Cardinals hat, but that was the only baseball paraphernalia she had brought with her this time. He decided to park in the main lot next to the stadium and was glad to see a small army of Cardinals fans walking through the lot to the ballpark. It was the third game of the year, and it appeared the local crowd had already begun to give way to fans from the visiting team. They had painted Shea a festive purplish color, but Nathan thought that it was a futile gesture. Shea would always be a charmless industrial structure shoehorned between railroad sidings and the Grand Central Expressway. Only when you stepped into the stadium were you graced with the sounds of baseball and greeted by the impossibly green outfield grass that barely seemed real given the state of their own lawn. When visiting stadiums, they always sat on the third base side so they could be near the visitor's dugout. In past years, they would try and get players' autographs before the game started. A few years ago, they were lucky enough to briefly talk to the Cardinals star shortstop Ozzie Smith. The Wizard of Oz. Given their conversation in the car today, Nathan was reticent to suggest that they try to obtain some autographs, so he just waited for Mira to tell him what she wanted to do. After a few minutes of silence, Nathan tried an innocent parry.

"Hot dog?"

"Do you know what's in those?"

"To be honest, I'd rather not think about it on game days. I thought you loved hot dogs."

"Not anymore. They're pretty gross."

"So, what do you want to eat?"

"I'm not hungry yet. Maybe popcorn?"

"That's not really a meal."

"I know what it is."

"Alright. Maybe vendors will come around soon."

Mira knew she was being a pain, but she couldn't help herself. She stared out at the field and wondered if she had missed some clues along the way. Had it been obvious that her father was cheating? Had she been part of it somehow? Had she met this woman? Was it some neighbor she knew? She decided it probably couldn't have been or they might have moved by now. Was it a cute young teacher at his school? That seemed the most likely scenario. She had noticed that the teachers gathered outside the local elementary school looked barely older than she was. Her father *was* charming. Even her friends said so. In truth, she suspected, not knowing was actually worse than knowing.

While she was pondering the other woman, the game had started. Her father was already telling the umpire he couldn't see straight after only the second pitch. A record for him. Mira couldn't really concentrate so she looked around the stadium and focused on the constant stream of planes buzzing overhead as they took off from nearby LaGuardia Airport. She wondered where they were going. Maybe someplace exotic? Shea was only about half full, and their row, which was close to the field, was largely unoccupied except for an older man and his son who was about her father's age. They were both wearing Mets hats which made Mira smile. The older man probably had donned his first baseball cap when he was a little boy and here he was stuffing his thinning gray hair into another one. The man's son looked over at Mira and noticed she was looking at his father.

"That hat of yours is going to cause trouble with my dad." He said with a grin on his face.

"Family obligation." Mira replied.

"Dad. You okay sitting in the vicinity of this pretty young lady with the Cards hat?"

His father stopped watching the game and looked over at Mira. She noticed his nose was colored purple.

"Depends who wins the game." He winked at Mira. Nathan was half listening to the conversation and watching the game. Mira didn't think he was listening at all, so she was surprised when he put his arm around her and told the old man that his daughter was going to marry a Cardinals fan many many years from now. They grinned and returned to watching the game, and Mira waited for Nathan to take his arm off of her. A few seconds later he placed it on the chair behind her, and she leaned over and asked him why he had cheated on Marian.

"What?"

"You heard me."

"I don't know what you think you know."

"I overheard you and Uncle Gordon."

"I don't know what you heard."

"Please don't make me repeat it. Why would you do something like that?"

Nathan realized now why she had been so distant the last few weeks. *Fucking Gordon.* Such a big mouth. Now he was going to fuck up the one perfect relationship he had ever had in his life.

"I don't know that this is the place to discuss this honey."

"You have a better place? I'm not sure I even want to know the details. I just want to know two things."

"What?"

"Is it true? And why would you do that to Mom?"

"If it makes you feel better it was a long, long time ago and your mother knows how sorry I am about what happened."

Nathan knew she was only asking about his infidelity with Ellen. He couldn't possibly tell her he had cheated on her mother when they were dating in college. An additional revelation would probably damage their relationship for years. He thought he could contain this breach because she probably wanted to believe whatever he told her.

"Were you unhappy? Were you going to leave Mom?"

"I *was* unhappy, but not with her. With myself. If that makes any sense. Can I ask you a really big favor?"

"What?"

"Can you not tell your mom we had this talk? It would reopen a very old wound."

Mira wasn't really good at keeping secrets, but she had no desire to hurt her mother.

"I guess so."

"Thank you. I'm so sorry you had to hear about this. It had nothing to do with you in any way. Like I said, it was all about me and my stupidity and selfishness."

"You keep saying that but you haven't explained why."

"It's the truth honey. Would your mother have taken me back otherwise?"

Mira didn't know what the truth was anymore. She looked over at the man with his father. He was leaning over so that his father could hear him and had his arm around him. What were their secrets? Did his father beat him with a strap? Drink too much? Whatever he did they were acting like best friends. How did people get past these things? She wanted to go back in time and forget she ever heard the whole conversation but she knew it was too late.

32

desire

Long ago, when she was thirty-one, Marian had written a poem about sexual desire. As she was leaning over and clipping her rosebush, she was thinking about that poem and felt her back start to seize up on her. She gingerly tried to straighten up before the spasm gripped her too tightly. She went inside and looked around for a hot water bottle she could apply to her back. She thought perhaps she had left it under the sink in the hall bathroom the last time Nathan had needed it. To her surprise, she located it behind a bath brush. At least, her memory was intact. She filled it with hot water, positioned herself upright in bed and placed it where the twinge had reached across her spine. She began to think about the poem again. She wrote it when she was a much younger woman and sex was less complicated. It might follow a mere knowing glance between them right before one of them shut the light or Nathan might catch a glimpse of her stepping out of the shower.

Sometimes, a gratifying meal paired with a bottle of their favorite Cabernet provided enough encouragement.

When her period began to wane, desire ceded ground to something more preordained. Would Nathan stray again if she didn't show the requisite interest? The thought had crossed her mind more than once. But sometimes all she wanted to do after that bottle of Cabernet was drift off to sleep. Nathan didn't complain as they became less amorous, but he would sometimes comment on her "lack of energy." So, when Charles suggested they go away for a long weekend, she tried to be as casual as possible, but her stomach was churning. As he ticked off potential destinations, she could only envision the king-sized bed, ready and made up, in each of the hotel rooms. She had seen pictures of Nathalie as a younger woman and she couldn't possibly measure up with any version of her. There was clearly a reason that Charles had wrested her away from her parents in France. She looked like she had stepped off the set of a Truffaut film.

∽

When Mira called last night, Marian couldn't quite bring herself to share that she was going away for the weekend with Charles. She just couldn't get past the optics and decided to be vague about her weekend plans. There was also something in Mira's voice that worried her. She said all the right things but her answers were a bit too rosy and her voice too high. Her daughter was always the hard-nosed realist and her descriptions were devoid of her typical analysis tinged with a dose of reality, or when warranted, sarcasm. She decided to try and put it out of her mind for the time being and try to enjoy herself with Charles.

She hadn't been to the Berkshires in years, so when Charles suggested Stockbridge for the weekend, it wasn't totally unappealing. She had been to Lenox for the wedding of a college friend of Nathan's. She remembered thinking this was a place she would like to return to, but they never did. When Nathan retired from teaching, they had gone on a few trips, and she foolishly thought there was time to retrace their steps. She had wanted to return to Greece to swim in the Mediterranean again and watch the sun from the cliffs of Io fill the sky at dusk. She had wanted to reacquaint herself with the sense of freedom she felt as she navigated scriptless through an unfamiliar city.

Marian looked over at Charles behind the wheel and smiled. Why was it that when she was twenty, she would have looked at this trip as a titillating journey and her relative unfamiliarity with him would have been intoxicating? Instead, her mind veered from the thrilling to the rather eerie thought of what would his dead wife share with her if she was a presence in the car? Turn back? His strong chin masks a weak constitution and he'll disappoint you? Perhaps, Charles yearned to consort with Nathan and ferret out all of *her* foibles? Amid the cognitive clutter, she managed to dismiss the thought. Men didn't seem to consume as much time as women pondering the past. Maybe that was healthier, but she couldn't shake the judgement that Santayana would have been sorely disappointed with the shortsightedness of most of the men she had dated.

"So, you said you've been here before?"
"Long time ago."
"With Nathan?"
"Yes. A wedding."
"No kids?"

"Not then."

"We used to come up here and do some cross-country skiing in the winter. It was one of the few activities we did as a family."

"Never skied."

"Never?"

"Neither of us grew up near mountains. I think Mira on occasion went skiing with her college friends."

"Nathalie also loved all the galleries up here. She liked the artsy feel of the whole area."

"It's funny you brought that up. I've been meaning to ask you."

"What's that?"

"Is that part of your connection to me? Painter. Poet."

"I honestly hadn't thought about it. At least not consciously. But I can see why you might think that."

"So, if I was a pharmacist, you would have tossed me aside already?"

"Very funny."

"I'm half serious."

"The funny thing is I was a business major, and I didn't spend a whole lot of time in libraries or museums growing up or for that matter, reading, much less considering literature."

"So why me?"

"I could ask you the same thing."

"You asked me out."

"Simple as that, huh?"

"Well, I think the young woman in me might have had something to do with it."

"She's still lurks in there," Charles said pointing to her heart.

"We'll find out."

The bed and breakfast was run by a couple of New York City refugees who had escaped the island. The wife was the chattier of the two and transitioned seamlessly to a first name basis with them by the time she finished checking them in. The room was a bit too Victorian for Marian with its poster bed frame and frilly coverings. She was drawn to a broad casement window that looked down on a garden which called for her to visit. Signs of spring were afoot and she loved to observe flowers as they began to bloom. Some years she took photos each day to try and capture the changes. There was a wooden bench in the garden that looked like a perfect place to write. She sensed that Charles had other things on his mind.

"Nice room. The pictures on the web site were spot on."

She felt him put his arms around her shoulders and neck. Marian flashed back to New Orleans for some reason. Was he going to try and pull off her clothes? She could smell his cologne as his beard grazed her cheek. She and Nathan were not perfume and cologne people. She turned and he kissed her with a firmness she hadn't experienced since Nathan and, as he held her, she could feel his hand pressed against the middle of her back. He had kissed her before, but this was something altogether different. He suddenly let her go and looked at her. She didn't know him well enough yet to discern what he was trying to convey, so she waited.

"I can wait."

"I enjoyed it."

"Yeah?"

"Yes."

"Let's go and explore."

"That sounds good."

She followed him out the door, and part of her wanted to tell him to come back and jump in that frilly old bed with her. But she needed some air and she had the whole weekend to change her mind. The chatty wife was talking to someone who was checking in, looked up, and smiled. She was probably wondering what they were doing downstairs already. Marian couldn't wait to get back in the car.

33

help

1997

They called it their blackest year. Nathan's father was never able to recover from the stroke, and he had been slipping away for months. Throughout 1997, Nathan drove I-95 so often he was sure cashiers at the Maryland House rest stop knew him by sight. As far as Nathan was concerned there was but one single silver lining. Mira was so concerned about her grandfather, she became his driving companion. He had never breathed a word of his conversation with Mira at Shea, but he wondered if Mira had shared anything with Marian. He knew Marian didn't like long car rides, but she would have come with him if he asked. It was almost like she sensed that the father-daughter relationship needed to be repaired. At first, there were long patches of silence the first few times they drove to Maryland. But, as Nathan's father deteriorated and they continued to make their somber journeys, an unspoken bond was forged. He knew Mira had never lost anyone so he tried to balance hope and reality. She was too old now to completely shield her.

It was late November and a freezing rain was falling as they made it to the car. Nathan grabbed the ice scraper from the trunk and cleaned the windshield. He could see how forlorn Mira was sitting there. Perhaps she sensed they would never see his father again. He was barely eating and it was a struggle for him to open his eyes. If Mira hadn't been in the room, his mother would have completely fallen apart. She had made them dinner. Then they talked about high school, Marian's latest book, and everything else they could think of except what was going on upstairs. Periodically, the live-in aide they hired would come downstairs and his mother would give her some guidance. Before they left after lunch the next day, Nathan talked to his mother privately and asked her if he should stay. She thanked him, but said she could get by with the help of the aide and Gordon was only fifteen minutes away if anything happened.

Nathan wiped off some of the glaze that had formed on the windshield and slid behind the wheel. He looked at Mira, who was now crying.

"Shouldn't we stay?" Mira said through tears.

"Grandma has help and Uncle Gordon is close by."

"Is he dying?"

What do you tell your sixteen-year-old daughter? Nathan asked himself. He was still trying to process seeing his father slipping away.

"I think so, honey. I think it may be a matter of days or weeks."

"It's so unfair."

"It is. He isn't an old man. At least, not to me anymore."

"What's grandma going to do? She'll be all alone in that big house."

"I'm not sure honey. It's a good question. She might stay there awhile until she can't manage anymore. We'll still come to Maryland and help her."

"Maybe we should move here."

"You would leave all your friends?"

Mira paused to consider the question. She didn't really like high school and felt like she was just biding her time until college anyhow.

"Yes."

"Wow."

"I would miss a few of them, but I'll be going to college in a year and a half anyhow."

Nathan started to say something, but he was so touched his daughter would move all the way to Maryland to take care of his mother that the words caught in his throat.

"Thank you."

"For what?"

"For offering to make that sacrifice."

He checked the road ahead and saw there were no cars coming and reached out and put his hand on her tear-streaked cheek. She didn't stop him.

"That means a lot to me. Especially because I know how upset you've been with me." She didn't respond, but he took her silence as a peace offering.

His father passed ten days later. Marian's mother called while they were at the funeral home and Nathan assumed she was calling to speak with his mother. Marian left the room and came back, her mascara running.

"What?"

"Christopher."

"Back in the hospital?"

"Gone."

"Gone?"

"She said his body couldn't take the chemo anymore. The doctor said his heart finally gave out."

"How is she?"

"Not good," she managed to say while crying.

"Maybe we should wait to say anything to anyone."

"I agree. My poor mom. She has to go through *this* all over again."

"He was a nice man."

"She deserved someone like him. How do you think Mira will react?"

Nathan looked over at where Mira was sitting with his mother with her arm around her.

"She'll be fine. Your daughter is something. Do you know she offered to move Maryland to be with my mother?"

"Just her?"

"No. All of us."

"She said that?"

"I forgot to tell you."

"What did you tell her?"

"I almost cried when she told me."

"She *is* something. Stronger than both of us put together."

"Our crowning achievement."

"What *are* we going to do about our mothers?"

"I don't know. I'm not moving to Maryland. And I assume Grand Rapids is not in our future either."

"One of them may need to live with us or near us."

"More likely to be your mother. Gordon lives close enough to keep tabs on my mom."

"Who knows if she'd come?"

"It's a long way from Grand Rapids to New York."

Nathan could see over Marian's shoulder that Carly Meyer had just entered the room and was coming over to where they were standing. One more complication. She hugged Nathan and he introduced her as an "old friend." She had to be close to fifty, but you would have never known it.

"I loved your dad. I'm so sorry."

"Thanks."

"My mom had told me about the stroke."

"He never really recovered."

"He always made me laugh. He was so funny and always made me feel welcome in your house."

"I'm sure my mom would love to hear that."

"Where is your mom?"

"She's over there sitting next to my daughter."

"Oh look at that. She's a beauty. 18?"

"Close. She's 17."

"I'm looking forward to meeting her. I think the last time I saw you she was about two. Time flies."

She turned toward Marian and offered her hand.

"I'm Carly Meyer. A friend of the family. Nice to meet you."

"Same here. Thanks for coming."

"Of course."

When she was out of earshot Marian turned to Nathan.

"Old girlfriend?"

"Very old. Like sixth grade or something."

"She remembered you pretty well. Pretty woman."

"Not bad."

"Funny thing is I don't recall seeing her when Mira was two."

"Yeah, I don't know when that was. Maybe she came by when we visited my parents?"

"I think I would remember an ex-girlfriend who looked like that."

"I don't know what to tell you."

He looked guilty of something. She wondered if it was actual guilt or if her perception was being guided by her persistent distrust of Nathan. She wasn't going to confront him at a funeral home and she didn't have any evidence anyhow. Just an uneasy feeling. She also couldn't recall when he had been to Maryland without her that long ago. It had been a long time since he had made her feel like she was the only person who wasn't fully aware of the truth. She'd thought she was done with this.

34

damaged

For a long time after his triple bypass the jagged scar was a bright red, but over time the hue changed to more of a rust color, and finally, it faded to a maroon stripe. Charles held his shirt in one hand and ran his fingers along the scar line with the other. He used to like taking his shirt off during the summer but now he covered himself up everywhere but the shower. When he asked Marian if she wanted to go away for the weekend, he was worried what she might say if she saw him without his shirt on. He hadn't told her about the surgery yet. Having lost her husband to a heart attack, he didn't know if she would be scared off by his medical history. When she seemed hesitant to make love, he was actually temporarily relieved that he wouldn't have to tell her his secret.

After his surgery, he only had sex with Nathalie a handful of times before she started feeling ill when her late stage cancer began to reveal itself. He hadn't told her that on each of those occasions he prayed that his heart wouldn't blow up in the middle of their lovemaking. He couldn't really concentrate because he kept focusing on his breathing and his own chest cavity. How was he going to explain all this to Marian? He wouldn't blame her if she didn't want damaged goods.

2017

The last thing that Nathalie remembered before her chemo dream was watching a cruise ship in the Hudson River slowly pull away from the dock. She could see people on the decks, some excitedly talking, others gazing at the City on their way to the Atlantic Ocean and places unknown. She had barely made it to the car from the hospital doors this time, and Charles had just enough strength to lift her into the seat. She had been worrying for weeks how Charles would fare without her if this latest round of chemo didn't work. Kristin was well on her way to creating a full life for herself and soon she would give birth. Henry was still alone but he had started to awaken from the distracted state that had absorbed him during his adolescent and teen years. Her son had never really made the transition from being attached to her to that connection that boys have with their fathers.

For some reason, she was always traveling in these dreams and the plane flights always seemed endless. Usually she would end up in strange places and this time she was standing by the side of the road next to a tour bus. There were trees bursting with green bananas on the side of a mountain, and everyone was looking down below at something. She was afraid of heights, but she walked up to the edge and looked down into the ravine. She wasn't sure what she was looking at, but someone grabbed her waist from behind. She turned to see Charles laughing and told him he wasn't funny. He apologized. She thought maybe she was in the Canary Islands or South America. The other passengers were all smoking by the side of the road. She told Charles to make them all stop and she turned over and saw that it was 4:00AM, and that she had been sleeping for hours.

Charles was snoring next to her and she could see his chest moving up and down. She had spent months worrying whether he would recover fully from his heart surgery, and now that seemed relatively trivial. Nathalie got up to wash her face and take off her makeup and realized she had to vomit. Charles called into the bathroom to ask if she was okay. She caught her breath and told him to go back to sleep. Trying to gather herself, she looked in the mirror to see her makeup was now running and filling in the deepening channels in her face. She wiped it off and splashed some cold water on her face. When she opened her eyes, Charles was standing behind her, and she thought she could smell lingering cigarette smoke from her dream.

"Throwing up?"

"Oui."

"Kristin called while you were out cold."

"What did you tell her?"

"That you were in dreamland."

"Can you help me back to bed?"

Charles practically had to carry her back to bed and propped up her pillows.

"This is the last time."

"We'll just take it as it comes."

"Three is the end. If it works, and they ask me to do a commercial for their miracle drug, then I'll dance a jig for them. But if it fails…" Nathalie's thought drifted off, but she didn't need to say any more.

"The oncologist said—"

"I know what he said. There's always another drug. But he only said that because you asked him."

Charles knew she was right, but he wasn't going to admit it. He needed to stand strong so that she wouldn't give up. He could see her slipping away. When she went through the chemo treatments, they seemed to eat away at her will to live.

"I want you to find someone."

"What are you talking about?"

"When I go."

"Stop."

"You need someone."

"I have the children."

"The children love you but that's not enough. They're adults now with their own lives."

He knew what she was omitting to spare his feelings. They loved her more. Who could blame them? Charles got back into bed and put his arm over her body. Her nightdress pulled back so he could see the bruises and scarring from her ports. Could he be as brave as her? He didn't think so. He was one of the best swimmers in his school, but his coach never let him anchor the relays. When he finally confronted the coach about his position, his coach told him that he was a fast starter, but if he needed someone to come from behind, he thought a few of the boys were "better fits." Charles knew what he meant. He didn't think he had the heart to finish strong and pass someone from far back. He didn't agree with him at the time, and when he went home that night, threw one of his trophies across the room where it gouged the wall. For years afterward he would touch the small hole in the wall if he needed to conjure up some righteous indignation.

Nathalie quickly fell back to sleep, and Charles pondered what she said about finding another woman. When he was seventeen, he always thought there was a better version of his latest girlfriend just around the corner. He used to do pushups next to his bed every night and took long loving looks at his biceps in the mirror before and after every shower. He no longer had any great desire to look in the mirror. Despite what she said, he wasn't sure what he had to offer any woman now. Even if he did find someone, how could he possibly avoid being haunted by the long shadow his marriage to Nathalie would cast? No, he couldn't allow these thoughts to weaken his resolve to help her survive. The consequences of failure were too enormous to fully contemplate. She just *had* to live. That's what he had to tell himself. The wall separating them from failure would have to be fortified somehow.

35

78 rpm

Marian wasn't sure if it was guilt or something else. She hadn't visited the cemetery in weeks. While trimming her New York ironweeds yesterday she envisioned the evergreen yews by Nathan's plot and wondered if they were overgrown. But when she went inside, she was dismayed to find black ants had invaded her kitchen again. She had tried vinegar last year to ward them off, but she only had limited success. Ultimately, she called in an exterminator. The man had talked confidently of "a guaranteed five-year solution," but that was clearly just a sales pitch. These ants were so persistent you would have thought they could survive a nuclear blast.

She impulsively smashed a number of them with her muddy shoe and then realized her sole was now a mixture of dirt and dead ants. She took off her shoes and laid them outside on the back porch to clean later. The phone rang just as she stepped back inside.

"When are you going to get a cell phone?"
"Mira?"
"Yes, your daughter. Who else would it be?"
"You sound angry."
"A little bit. At myself, mostly."
"What's going on?"
"Are you sitting down?"
"Yes."
Marian leaned against the back door.
"I'm pregnant."
"Pregnant. Are you sure?"
"Do you think I'd call you if I wasn't sure?"
"I guess not. It was an…accident?"
"Yes, of course."
"Well, people do all kinds of things these days."
"Well, this wasn't one of those things."
"Matt?"
"He doesn't want it. I mean he didn't say it that way of course, but he fumbled about for words after I told him."

Not surprising. That boy never seemed to want any responsibility.

"It?"
"You know what I mean."
"How far?"
"Ten weeks."
"What are you going to do?"
"I really don't know."
"Do you want me to come out to Seattle?"
"And do what? No."
"Do you want my advice?"

"Maybe."

"I know you like children."

"Other people's."

Marian hadn't allowed herself to think too much about what it might be like to be a grandmother. She saw herself holding a baby, and it made her smile.

"When it's yours, it's different. Trust me."

"What if he leaves? I'll be a single mom."

"If he leaves before that baby is born, then he doesn't deserve you."

"Some people just don't want to be parents. You only had one child."

"And I regret it."

"That's sweet."

"Mira."

"Kidding."

"Have you been to the doctor?"

"I have an appointment."

"Take your time. That's my advice. I know your brain must feel like it's on 78 rpm."

"78 what?"

"Metaphorically. Your head is spinning fast."

"Oh. Yeah."

"Are you feeling okay?"

"For the most part. The nausea seems to have passed."

"You're lucky."

"That's me. Lucky."

"If you want me to come, just say the word."

"I know. I'll call you tomorrow."

"Goodnight sweetie."

Marian wanted to jump through the phone line and hug Mira. Was she encouraging enough? Maybe she should have been more direct about keeping the baby. Mira never was one to respond well to pressure, so she thought it was best to act like there wasn't really a crisis. She was dying to jump on a plane and sit next to her for twenty-eight weeks to wait for that baby to open its eyes. It reminded her of a poem she wrote after she had a miscarriage and before Mira was born.

We mourned
for your sister
who would never speak
there were no new sounds
just a room
some yellow paint
a mobile of twirling stars and
a rocking horse
an heirloom
from mother
so we waited
for you to come
yellow became lavender
a mobile became a mural
only the rocking horse
remained
to remind us of the rides
she would never take

Marian hadn't thought about the miscarriage in a long time. She didn't believe in the power of dark thoughts, crossing her fingers, and other silly superstitions. Her parents had drummed those out of her at a young age. Maybe she was thinking about it because her daughter had raised the specter of an abortion, probably because of Matt's selfishness. Marian thought that after you'd been with someone for a long time you had to accept certain risks, and this was certainly one of them. She knew better than most that love wasn't some straight line. Mira probably would stay up all night and watch that boyfriend of hers sleep like the dead. Nathan had been the same way after she lost the baby. Though she couldn't fault him, he drove her to the hospital and held her hand and wiped her tears. But when they came home that night, he fell right to sleep while she didn't sleep more than an hour that night slumped in a chair in the baby's room.

Marian had been sitting in the kitchen, and it occurred to her that her grandmother's rocking horse was in the attic. When Mira was around eight, she insisted they take it out of her room. Nathan had brought it up into the attic where it was gathering dust. She wasn't superstitious, but she thought she better wait until she heard more news from Seattle before she offered it to Mira. She wondered where that mobile was too. She couldn't bring herself to throw it out or use it again.

36

cruising

2017

*N*athan had been asking her to go on a cruise for the longest time. But the idea of being shoe horned in a confined space with thousands of strangers, and on the ocean no less, was wholly unappealing to Marian. She finally agreed to go on the cruise after Nathan suggested a relatively short one to Bermuda. However, it was not before she confirmed no hurricanes were hiding far out in the Atlantic and made him book a large cabin since she had heard horror stories about how tiny the cabins were on these ships. Much to her chagrin, it turned out that "large" really meant rather small but not tiny. Nathan agreed it was "a bit cozier" than he expected, but at least they had a sizable window to alleviate some of her claustrophobia. Marian found the little window far from comforting.

As she stood on the top deck and they passed the Statue of Liberty, she traced it in the air and then put her hand around Lady Liberty. Nathan asked her what she was doing and she said she was drawing. He leaned over and kissed her. Then, he took his phone and asked her to pose for a bon voyage photo. She obliged, and they looked at the picture. She saw an old lady staring back at her. When she looked up, they were passing Ellis Island, and all the people around them were taking photos with their phones. Nathan said he was pretty sure his mother's family had come through Ellis Island from Scotland.

Nathan suggested they go down to the pool when the ship left the Hudson and headed out to the ocean. Marian thought it sounded ridiculous to sit by a pool on a ship, but she knew what she had signed up for, so she agreed. To her surprise the pool area was spacious enough and was built below the deck so that you forgot you were on a ship after a while.

"Nice huh?"

"I have to admit."

"See. We could become cruisers after all."

"I wouldn't press your luck just yet. We'll see if there any icebergs in our way or rotavirus outbreaks."

"You're the only iceberg around here." He smiled, and even though his face was no longer smooth, his dimples underneath that baseball hat still travelled a direct path to her heart.

"Hah."

"I'm available for applying suntan lotion."

"I'm sure you are. I think I'll keep my shirt on. The sun is going to go down soon."

"I wonder why these ships leave so late in the afternoon. Must save them money or something."

"Mira called this morning."

"How is my princess?"

"She said you called last night."

"I figured she forgot we were going away."

"I told her to water my flowers and collect the newspapers."

"We can't complain."

"About her?"

"She may not be a star like her mother, but she's someone I would want to know even if she wasn't my daughter."

"I like the way you put that, says the star," Marian said while grinning.

"I heard there's something like eight restaurants on this boat."

"Ship." Marian wiggled her toes and noticed that she really needed a pedicure.

"If you prefer."

"I think I'm going to get a pedicure before dinner. We passed a salon on the way down here."

"Luxuriate, my dear. Luxuriate."

When the sun started to go down, Marian told Nathan she would meet him back at the room, provided she could find it. She began to notice that the people on the ship were not exactly suburbanites. At the nail salon there were a lot of women talking to each other with thick New York accents. Two younger women were having a long discussion about someone named Lady Gaga. She sounded like a performer of some kind. Marian recalled when Mira used to wear those flannel shirts and listened to that awful loud music. That marked the last time she had any knowledge of what kids of her generation were listening to. The woman at the nail salon convinced her to have her nails painted after she finished with her toes. She usually thought it was a waste of time since she knew when she gardened the polish would invariably quickly chip off. But she wanted to surprise Nathan, and she thought it might last longer on the ship.

On the way back to the room, Marian thought maybe she would surprise Nathan tonight and initiate their lovemaking. Maybe if he wasn't famished, then she might close the lights when she got back. She might be too tired by the time they got back from a late dinner. She knocked but there was no answer so she tried her key card and found Nathan on the floor next to the bed. His mouth was open and he was perfectly still. It took a few moments for her to realize that he wasn't breathing. Terrified she ran out of the room, screamed, and then ran back into the room to see if anything had changed. He hadn't moved. So, she ran back out of the room and almost ran into an older man in a sports jacket who said he had called for help and asked her what was wrong.

"He's not moving. My husband."

The man kneeled down next to Nathan and felt his neck and wrist and looked up. Before he could say anything a doctor in a white coat came into the room and started CPR. Marian watched as he rhythmically pounded on Nathan's chest which caused Nathan's body to move, giving the illusion that he was alive. A woman, presumably a nurse came in. They used paddles on his chest to try and shock him back to life with a defibrillator. Nothing worked. Marian thought she was going to pass out when the doctor got off his knees to speak with her. She heard nothing. He guided her to the bed and sat next to her. He couldn't have been much older than Mira. She focused on a mole he had over his lip as his mouth moved. She realized he said he would speak to the captain but never heard what he was going to say to the captain. After that, she couldn't remember anything else he said. The man in the sports jacket who had called the doctor stood over them with his hand over his mouth. The nurse found a towel and placed it over Nathan's bare chest. Marian didn't understand why. The doctor reached into his bag and pulled out a bottle and asked Marian if she wanted something to relax her. She thought his use of the word "relax" was ironic, but she agreed and took one of the pills he handed her.

Marian didn't know how much time passed, but the people in the room changed. The man with the jacket was gone. A man, who appeared to be the captain was standing there commiserating with her. She heard him say, "arrangements in port." She just nodded. At some point, he left. Then the doctor took his leave after checking her blood pressure. The nurse remained in case Marian needed anything. She explained that protocol was that she wait with "the body" until it was taken below deck. Marian was slumped in a chair now, feeling exhausted. She could feel her own weight pressing against the armrest. She nodded off and when she awoke Nathan's body was gone. Just like that. The nurse was still sitting there and she smiled wanly when Marian opened her eyes. She had an overwhelming urge to speak with Nathan.

"Where's my husband?" She could barely hear her own voice.

"Below deck."

"Are we going to Bermuda?"

"Yes."

"How long until we get there?"

"About 36 hours from now. They asked me if you have any special requests regarding burial rituals."

"Burial rituals? Who asked? You're not burying him there are you?"

"No, of course not. Just in terms of preparing him."

"No. No special rituals."

"I'll let them know. I am so sorry about all this."

"Thank you."

Marian told the nurse; whose name was Gretchen that she could go. She told Marian she would check on her later. Gretchen couldn't leave the room fast enough.

Marian was completely alone. She never expected to be alone on the cruise. She stared at the floor. There were some cotton swabs sticking out from under the bed. They were the only sign she wasn't dreaming and that he wouldn't just walk out of the shower or knock on the door at any moment. Still exhausted, she knelt down to pick them up. Doubling over, she started crying until her throat was raw and her stomach muscles felt as if they would tear apart. She composed herself and thought that while she was getting her toenails painted, Nathan was dying in this cabin. What was she thinking? She didn't even like getting her nails done. Maybe she could have saved him. She knew she had to call Mira, but how she could she ever tell her that her father was gone? The carpet was starting to dig into her knees, and so she fell to one side and leaned against the bed. His baseball hat was sitting on the night table. She wanted to bring it to him to keep him company.

37

boy

Mira walked outside the doctor's office and looked up when she felt a raindrop. There was a single black cloud in the sky, which made her smile. She never had any patience for people who ascribed their day to day existence to luck. But if anyone was owed some luck, it was her. Her father had been suddenly taken away from her and now she was pregnant thousands of miles from home.

A boy. She wasn't prepared when the nurse asked her if she wanted to know the sex of the baby. She had such an inviting smile that she didn't want to disappoint her, so she said okay. As a child, she wanted her parents to have a boy so she could have a little brother to play with and boss around. But what did she know about raising boys? If her boyfriend was typical, then she would need to find the self-control to let go of her desire to remake this child in her image.

Mira retraced her steps to the bus stop a few blocks away

and sat down on a bench. She opened her purse and pulled out her compact to check her makeup. She thought maybe she had teared up in the examination room, but it didn't look like her mascara had run. She started to put her compact back and noticed the Mariners' baseball schedule sticking out of her pocketbook. She had picked it up reflexively at a supermarket, even though Matt wasn't much of a sports fan. Her father would have probably expressed his displeasure that she had moved to an American League city, but then he would have laughed. He didn't even like inter-league play and boycotted any Cardinals games at American League parks. He told her he would wait until the World Series to see his beloved Cardinals play one of those teams.

She pulled out the schedule and smiled. The Cardinals were coming to Seattle in June. She desperately wanted to call her father to convince him to fly out to see her, but just as she imagined his face, she heard the bus coming and looked up. With tears in her eyes, she noticed an advertisement for opening day tickets on the side of the bus. She boarded the bus and an old lady smiled at her, as if she could see right through her. Mira started rubbing her belly, and she felt her son move. Or maybe it was just her imagination. *Her son.* She knew in his heart of hearts; her father was fully expecting his baby to be a boy when she emerged thirty-two years ago. But he never once made her feel she was less than what he wanted in a child. Now, in some cruel twist of fate, she would be bearing the male grandchild he would have adored, but would never meet.

~

When her mother insisted on coming to see her, Mira planned the trip so they could go to the ballpark and see the Cardinals.

Her mother didn't protest even though Mira knew she had no interest in baseball. Never did. When they sat down, she could see why people compared it to other stadiums. It was one of those "retro" stadiums recreating the unconventional angles of old stadiums which was all the rage in baseball architecture. Most of these stadiums had fan friendly areas that melded with the surrounding neighborhood. She thought back to when she was eleven, and her father rushed into her room one day, and breathlessly informed her that they were taking a road trip to someplace called Camden Yards. At the time, she wondered what it was.

"Is it a park?"

"Oh yeah. A baseball park."

"Where is it?"

"Baltimore. In Maryland."

"Near Grandpa's?"

"Very close."

"Is he coming?"

"Yes. Just the three of us."

"Soon?"

"In a few weeks. They just built it. It looks like an old park. But new."

"Why would they want it to look old?"

"History. Baseball is all about history. It's supposed to make you feel as if you're part of history. Like Babe Ruth could have just played there. He grew up in Baltimore."

"I thought he was a Yankee." Mira grinned.

"Smart aleck." Nathan tickled her.

"Get off." She protested while giggling.

Mira closed her eyes, and for all the world she felt like he was tickling her again. She opened her eyes and realized it was just the baby moving in her womb. She settled into her seat and thought her father would have loved this park. His beloved Cardinals were throwing warm-up tosses to each other. She waited for him to start telling her something new about one of the players and turned to see her mother eating popcorn. Marian could see that she had a strange look on her face. Watching but not seeing.

"You feeling okay?"

"Yes, mother."

"Good. You know your father used to drag me to games when we were dating."

"I guess that's not surprising."

"I feigned interest for a while. But he knew I wasn't all that interested. Except for the popcorn."

She held up the popcorn and smiled.

"Can I ask you something?"

"Of course."

"Do you think I'm an idiot?"

"An idiot?"

"For having this baby."

"No, of course not."

"Who's going to hire a pregnant woman? I may be working at a bookstore for a very long time."

"You'll figure it out. I have faith in you."

When Marian caught a glimpse of Mira in the airport yesterday, she had to pull herself together. Her daughter, who was five years old just yesterday, was luminous and pregnant. She reflexively placed her hand on her own midriff, as if she was pregnant again. There were so many memories rushing through her mind. She was afraid she was going to fall apart right there in the airport, so she stopped before Mira saw her and then started walking when she regained her composure. Sitting next to her now she just wanted to grab her, hold her, and shelter her. But she resisted. She changed the subject.

"I know I'm just a substitute."

"Mom."

"This was *his* thing with you. It combined the two things he loved most in the world."

"I think *you* were in there somewhere."

"Yes, but this." Marian made a gesture toward the field. "To Nathan, this was pure and innocent. So were you as far as he was concerned. He and I were a little more complicated. Adults always are."

"He adored you."

"Maybe. I know I adored him ever since he walked across that coffee table."

"Coffee table?"

"We were drunk. Or a little high. Or both. But he was interested in me, and that's all that mattered at the time."

"So that's the key?"

"What's that?"

"Alcohol."

"It didn't hurt. Not sure I would recommend it."

"It's gotten me in trouble a few times." Mira patted her stomach and smiled.

"Following in my footsteps. I wouldn't use me as a role model."

"You're silly. I have something to tell you."

"Okay."

"I sort of told you a little white lie about the baby."

"What was that?"

Marian couldn't take any bad news. But she was smiling.

"I know the sex."

"You do? What are you trying to do to me Mira?"

"It's a boy."

"I had a feeling. I don't know why."

"And this is his first baseball game."

"I guess that's true."

They both stopped talking and looked toward the field in silence and settled back in their seats. Mira knew exactly what her mother was thinking. A few minutes later the national anthem was played, and they sat back down. As they sat down her mother rested her hand on Mira's knee and left it there. Mira put her hand on top of her mother's and they sat there watching the rest of the first inning that way.

38

paris

*B*etween the double panes and the raindrops sticking to the window, Marian could barely see the descent. The pilot had done his level best to direct them through the menacing black clouds that hung above Charles de Gaulle Airport, but the plane was still shuddering and rocking. Marian tried to think about Paris and not the landing. She didn't even realize how hard she was gripping Charles hand until he told her they would be on the runway soon enough.

Charles looked different to her now. Kinder. A little less opaque. A few months ago, when they had finally made love, she saw a more vulnerable man. She could see how concerned he was with the bypass scar that travelled across the better part of his torso. She had made a joke about her gallbladder scar and how they were certainly a matched pair. That seemed to calm him and her fears about her own potential inadequacies subsided to a degree.

Although she wasn't all that interested in travelling overseas anymore, she felt like she couldn't disappoint him when he asked her if she would go to Paris with him on a "minor business trip." She hadn't visited Paris in decades. Lengthy book tours had smothered her desire to travel long distances. Planes were never pleasurable when she was younger and even less so these days with all the fits and starts at airports. Who wanted to reveal your bare feet to perfect strangers and be subjected to searches? But she could see how excited he was leading up to the trip, so she steeled herself for the indignities she would have to endure.

The plane felt as if it was fishtailing on the damp runway but finally lurched to a stop. Charles hadn't shared with her where they were staying and kept saying it was a surprise. The taxi deposited them on the curb of a grand hotel in the shadow of the Eiffel Tower.

In another life she would have expected Nathan to close the room door and ask her to "try out the room" as he was wont to say. Now all she wanted to do was take a nap since it was morning in Paris and her brain still thought it was the middle of the night. Luckily, Charles was as tuckered out as she was, and they fell asleep until the sun began to fill the room through a break in the curtains. She had fallen asleep in her clothes and woke up in a sweat, so she went into the bathroom and threw some cold water on her face and instinctively looked up. She was still getting used to not seeing Nathan looming behind her in the mirror. He loved to sneak in and surprise her and grab her around the waist, even though he knew she despised being frightened. Somehow, he would always time it perfectly. No matter how many times she told him he was going to give her a heart attack, he would just laugh.

Marian tried to squeeze herself between the curtains without disturbing them and waking Charles. She gingerly opened the veranda door and stepped outside. The Eiffel Tower was so close she extended her hand and imagined touching the top with her finger. She felt hands on her waist and turned. It wasn't Nathan.

"Scared you?"

"I thought you were still sleeping."

"I heard the water."

"Oh, sorry."

"That's okay. We don't want to sleep the day away in Paris."

"I don't think we're close enough to the Tower."

"Thought you might like the view. We never tired of it."

"You mean I."

"That's what I said."

"No, you said *we*."

"I did? Sorry. Old habits."

"So, I'm not the first girl at the rodeo, eh?"

"Been to a rodeo?"

"Not on my bucket list, to be honest."

"I did ride one of those mechanical bulls once."

"That's something I'd pay to see."

"It wasn't pretty."

"So, do we have any more surprises for today?"

"Well, there is someone I wanted to visit while we're here."

"Nathalie's family?" She had wondered if they were going to be part of this trip.

"Good guess. No, they're not here in Paris. Not sure they'd want to see me anyhow."

"I doubt that."

"You'd be surprised then. I took away their daughter. I can't say that I blame them. And her father and I weren't exactly close."

"Lots of people move away. I did. My mother got over it. Sort of."

"It's not the same. The French are open minded about certain things, but her parents couldn't understand why she would want to leave France and them, of course."

"That's unfortunate."

"Well, I got what I wanted, so I can't complain too much."

"So, what's the *minor business* part of this trip?"

"Well, it's sort of business. There's a wine distributor here who was very important to my success and she's dying."

"Are you still in touch?"

"Not really, but her son still runs the business and he mentioned it to Henry. He knew how much she meant to my business, so he let me know. I was trying to calculate her age on the plane. She must be close to 95."

"What's her name?"

"Isabelle. Angelles. Quite the formidable woman in her day. She scared the hell out of me."

"Does she know you're here?"

"I don't know. I think she's pretty out of it from what I understand."

"Do you want to go alone?"

"I'm sure she would be happy to meet you. But, if you would rather explore on your own for a few hours, then that's fine, too."

Marian still didn't know Charles well enough to read the tea leaves and figure out when he was hedging the truth. They hadn't broken through that wall completely when you felt it was safe to reveal your darker angels. Clearly this woman meant something significant to him. Was it just a business relationship? She couldn't deny it was intriguing, and she might learn more about his past and him.

"I'd be happy to go."

"You sure?"

"If she meant something to you, then I am sure I'd like to meet her. I like formidable women." Marian smiled.

"Okay then. I don't want this to interfere with our adventures, so let's go after lunch. Shouldn't take too long."

"It's a date."

―⁓―

The African woman who opened the door looked surprised and didn't say anything for a few moments until Charles put out his hand and introduced himself. He explained that he was a long-time business associate of Isabelle. Marian just stood there trying to smile for as long as she could. She said her name was Yasmine.

"Madame Angelle is not well, I am afraid."

"We've come a long way. Is she awake?"

The woman stood there studying them.

"Bernard knows we were planning to visit." Charles added.

Her expression brightened immediately.

"Ah. Bernard. I will see if she is awake."

Charles expected a much larger apartment, even though he knew space was not easy to come by in Paris. The dark and heavy furniture made the living room seem claustrophobic. He looked for evidence of Isabelle's vocation, but there were just a few bottles of Bordeaux next to some artificial flowers perched on a side table. The curtains were mostly drawn but the windows provided enough light so that he could see that a layer of dust had settled in for what looked like a long residence.

After a few minutes, Yasmine came out and said she was ready to see them. When they walked into her bedroom, she was sitting hunched over in a wheelchair with oxygen prongs under her nose and a tank next to her bed. Even though her hair was completely white and her skin was pulling her face toward the floor, he could see she still had those steely gray blue eyes that always seemed to bore through him. She motioned him over and kissed him on both cheeks and he stepped back.

"Charles."

"Yes, Isabelle?"

Isabelle looked over at Marian and then looked back at Charles. He wasn't sure if her face registered confusion or alarm.

"Nathalie?"

"Gone, I'm afraid. Last year. Cancer. This is my friend, Marian."

He could see she was processing what he had told her. He thought he saw a tear and she drew a deep breath. Yasmine, who was sitting in the corner in a wing chair reading a book, looked up and then walked over and placed her hand on her shoulder. Isabelle's thin, mottled hand, shooed her back to her chair.

In her eyes and the stiffening of her posture, Charles could see a flash of the strong-willed woman he knew. He knew what was coming. "Why didn't you tell me she was ill?" Isabelle said emphatically.

"I don't know honestly." Although he didn't move, Charles could almost sense his chin dropping toward his chest. "I'm sorry. It seemed to happen so quickly. I was… in a fog."

"It's not supposed to be." She said wistfully.

"What's that?"

"I'm not supposed to be here. She is."

"I don't think she would say that. She adored you. You were like family."

"My poor Nathalie." Charles looked away as tears snaked their way silently down Isabelle's cheeks. Her words floated in the air. No one said anything for what seemed like an eternity. Charles looked over to Marian who had an expression on her face he couldn't decipher. Charles tried to change the subject.

"Well, Bernard and Henry have become friends. You see what you started?"

"More you than me."

"We did it together. I still don't know why you trusted me."

She motioned him over and he leaned in. "Si beau," she said. Charles laughed, and Isabelle's face seemed to come alive for a moment before settling back. He looked over at Marian, who didn't understand.

"She said it was because I was handsome."

"Ah."

Marian looked at Isabelle and nodded in agreement. Isabelle began to cough, and Yasmine came over with a bone white cloth to put up to her mouth.

"I think she is tiring." Yasmine said softly.

"We'll go now."

Charles went over to Isabelle and took her hand and held it for a moment.

"Good to see you my friend."

Marian wasn't sure, but she thought Isabelle nodded in her direction. Her eyes were beginning to close. Yasmine got up and began to lift her back into bed as they walked toward the door.

THE WIDOW *Verses*

When they got outside, Charles stopped and looked back at the building.

"I guess that's it."

"I guess so."

"I hope that wasn't too awful for you."

"It was fine. I don't have the same personal connections that you do. She clearly was very fond of you."

"I met Nathalie in her office. Sitting there reading some art history books."

"I see. You know it hasn't been that long." Marian was putting all the pieces together now. This "minor business trip" was nothing of the sort. This trip was as personal as it gets. Charles was here to see a piece of their history before it was gone.

"What?"

"Her passing. It's okay to still grieve. I know you want to move forward in that Charles way of yours. Stiff upper lip. That's partly why we're here. Nathalie may be gone but Isabelle was the beginning."

"I can't say you're wrong. I'm sorry."

"There's nothing to be sorry about."

Charles took Marian's hand, and she could see he wanted to avert his eyes from her so they began to walk. She understood now that she had been witness to a link that had now been severed.

39

sanibel

Marian and the sun always had an uneasy relationship. She knew her flowers required sun to thrive, but her fair skin did not appreciate the attention even with sunscreen and a wide-brimmed hat. Nathan had cajoled her into taking Mira to Disney one year, and she couldn't wait for each day to end. Mira had never been enamored of princesses, and so instead, she was forced to take her on roller coasters and water rides. She tried to beg off some of them but Mira was adamant. Nathan seemed to take perverse pleasure in her discomfort. She pouted most of that week. She didn't even mind that Mira slept between them during that week because she was too exhausted to make love.

Marian had no interest in returning to Florida until Charles mentioned it. Mira was on her mind almost all the time now. She was in her eighth month and last night she sounded beaten down. She was waking up to go to the bathroom during the night and sleeping less and less. When she told Mira she was going to Sanibel Island for the week, she didn't sound very enthusiastic and didn't ask any questions. She knew Mira wasn't swimming in money, but she knew she was too proud to ask her for anything. Since she met Charles she had taken more elaborate vacations, and even though she had paid her own airfares, she limited her recounting of the trips. She felt a little funny telling her daughter, who was living in a studio apartment with her penniless boyfriend about her adventures.

When they reached the causeway in their rental car, Marian resolved she was going to find some way to convince Mira to take some of the insurance money she had received last year after Nathan died. Maybe she would call it a baby present of some sort. The bridge seemed endless as it pierced the aqua blue water. There were just a few lazy clouds in the sky and she glanced at the Florida sun and shielded her eyes. Charles had taken his family to Sanibel a few times and said they had fallen in love with the beaches with its exotic shells and the ambiance of the island. She wondered if he even realized he was taking Marian on a greatest hits tour of his family vacations. Marian figured this was another unconscious way of saying goodbye to Nathalie. She had considered telling him they needed to create something that was unique to them, but she decided to wait it out. Since she still wasn't sure what she ultimately wanted, there was no need to push him to satisfy her own ego.

When Charles mentioned something about trees, she had no idea that driving through Sanibel was like traversing an enchanted forest. The trees snaked across the sky and hung over the road so completely the searing Florida sun was nearly obscured, as if a solar eclipse had occurred. Marian half expected a mythical creature to escape the trees and leap into the roadway. She craned her head and tried to get a better angle.

"You didn't tell me it was like *this*? It's almost... spooky."

"I mentioned them, didn't I?"

"Barely."

"She—" he stopped himself before he spoke her name.

"Now I see the allure of this place. It's as if you've completely left the banal wasteland of Florida."

"That's a bit harsh. And you haven't even seen the beaches."

~

1980

"We have nothing like this in Europe."

He loved how she said *Europe* with her accent, as if it was the most exotic place on earth. Nathalie bent over to pick up a shell, and he gently patted her bottom which he was caressing in bed an hour ago. He was starting to feel an erection coming on and tried to look away. It wasn't easy.

"There's something about the shape of this island that apparently acts like a funnel."

"Look at this one."

Charles looked at the shell, which was really two shells that had somehow fused together. He kissed her just because. He wasn't sure how long he could stay out of the bedroom. They spent the rest of the afternoon on the beach and Charles fell asleep at one point until a little girl with pigtails stepped on his towel. Nathalie laughed as the little girl stared at Charles and then picked up the ball her brother had thrown. Nathalie was only 24 but he could tell that she was already envisioning what her children might look like someday. Charles was used to negotiating prices and he had a feeling someday he might have to agree to have at least one child.

The next morning, he woke up and realized the little girl with pigtails had invaded his dreams. He had been holding her hand and walking somewhere. He remembered how small her hand seemed, and he had difficulty gripping it. Every time their hands unclasped, she would look at him and wait for him to take her hand again. Nathalie was still sleeping and the covers had slipped down and he could see her breasts moving as she breathed. He reached around and placed his hand in the space where her hip curved downward and moved closer to her. Who was he kidding? He was in so deep that he would agree to walk around the streets of New York in a clown suit if she asked him with that bewitching smile of hers. He leaned over and saw it was only eight o'clock in the morning. His parents had drilled into him that getting up late was a mortal sin. But these days he didn't really care about time anymore.

∽

Marian opened one of the drawers she had designated for her clothes and pulled out the bathing suit. She had bought it for the cruise to Bermuda but never wore it. It was the first bathing suit she had purchased in years and she had been looking forward to Nathan's reaction. She must have tried on twenty-five suits before settling on the black one she held in her hands. She had desperately wanted to ask one of the young women who worked at the store if she liked it on her, but she had been too embarrassed. Now, in the bathroom she put it on and looked in the mirror. It still seemed to fit pretty well, and she put her arms behind her head and held up her hair like a swimsuit model and turned to look at her profile from one side and then the other. Charles knocked at the door and she turned and let him in.

"I like it."

"Not too sexy?"

"I like sexy."

"You know what I mean."

"No. It's fine. Better than fine."

"Stop."

It was early June so the beaches weren't very crowded anymore. It was just after breakfast but the temperature was already rising toward ninety. Marian hoped her oversized floppy hat and cover up would protect her. Charles had checked the tide charts and assured her high tide was coming in with its bounty of shells. She didn't have the heart to tell him that she wasn't really a beach person. She never wanted to be one of those people who collected things, so that after she passed someone would be burdened with getting rid of all her junk. Funny thing, she hadn't really perceived Charles as a collector either.

The beach was a short walk from their condo and the sun was so bright she had to quickly put on her sunglasses. Charles didn't seem to mind the heat and seemed like a man on a mission. When they made it to the beach, Marian stopped. She wasn't sure what she was looking at. At first, she thought that there were sea creatures huddled together on the beach. There were maybe five feet of visible sandy shoreline and the rest of the beach was littered with mostly white shells.

"I told you." Charles could see her dumbfounded expression.
"I've never."
"Crazy, right?"
They set down their chairs on the thin strip of sand by the water and walked back into the shells. There were people with all sorts of containers scooping them up. She wondered what shells they were all looking for? She saw a little boy talking to his mother and thought about Mira. What time was it back in Seattle? She was probably sleeping right now. After about twenty minutes, Marian sat down in her chair and noticed that a man wearing a red baseball hat and a woman wearing a bathing suit that left little to the imagination had laid their blankets down nearby. It wasn't a Cardinals hat, but it still transported her back to the cruise ship. She looked over at Charles who was sifting through shells he had picked up. She had the ephemeral sense she wasn't supposed to be sitting next to this man. She immediately felt guilty and rested her hand on his arm. He looked up and smiled.

"What?"

"Thanks for taking me here."

"You're welcome."

"You're a good man."

"There are better. But thanks."

"I never told you, but my husband cheated on me and we were separated for a while at one point. So, I'm painfully aware that no one is perfect."

"I'm not sure what to say."

"Don't worry. I made my peace with it a long time ago."

Charles could see his instincts were right about her. She was strong. He felt the need to share something too.

"Nathalie took the kids to France for nine months one year when she was homesick. I have to admit I had some weak moments. It wasn't easy."

"What convinced her to move back?"

"I wish I could say it was my charm and strong chin, but I think it was harder than she thought it would be to go home after all those years. If you knew her father then you'd know what I'm talking about."

"I'm sure that was hard."

"It was a long time ago. We moved past it."

Marian decided to leave it alone. He didn't ask any more questions about Nathan's infidelity. She turned towards the water and closed her eyes. She imagined Nathalie getting off the plane after those nine months in France and how Charles must have felt standing there watching his wife and kids walking towards him. She remembered Nathan's expression when she let him in that night. As if he had been released from prison.

40

vassar

When Marian was much younger, on occasion, she would accept invitations to speak at poetry conferences, particularly if the invite came with all expenses paid and a stipend. She didn't really like giving speeches, but Nathan loved to travel. They would turn these invitations into explorations of states or countries they wouldn't have ordinarily visited. Estonia, Lebanon, South Africa, and New Zealand provided entry points to some of the most fascinating places she had ever seen. But as time went by and Nathan's knees began to go, they rarely accepted invitations.

"Why did I decide to become a catcher Marian?" he would ask wistfully. His years of crouching behind the plate in his youth had taken their toll and he had not warmed to his doctor's recommendations to have his knees replaced. He thought It sounded like something out of a sci-fi novel and he would end up worse after surgery.

So, when Marian opened a letter from Vassar inviting her to be one of the keynote speakers at a Fall Poetry Conference, she didn't give it much thought. In the days that followed, she thought about the time she visited Vassar as a high school student. She was so taken with the campus, she nearly attended college there. The mid-October conference would occur just when the autumn leaves would be at their most vivid in upstate New York, so she re-considered the invitation. She wasn't much of a driver, but she estimated it was only about an hour from her house. Deciding she would accept the invitation, she picked up the phone and before she changed her mind, called the contact in the letter.

Marian considered inviting Charles to the conference, but thought she would be much too busy talking with her fellow conferees, and, after all, it really wasn't his cup of tea. A few days before the conference she told him she would be away for the weekend.

"Away?"

"At a poetry conference up at Vassar. I barely considered attending when I received the invitation but impulsively decided to accept yesterday."

"Vassar. Impressive."

"It's quite a campus."

"Never been. I'll take your word for it."

"I almost went to school there. I think it was a little too artsy for my parents."

"How long will you be gone?"

Charles was dying to ask her why she hadn't invited him or told him about this until now, but he didn't want to seem "clingy" as his kids might say. He thought back to last Saturday night when they went out to dinner. He couldn't remember anything out of the ordinary, though she did have him drop her off after dinner.

"Just a few days. I'll call you when I get back."

"Enjoy."

Marian hung up and felt a bit guilty. Should she have invited him? He sounded taken aback on the phone. She walked outside on to her back deck and surveyed her backyard. The tree swing Nathan had constructed for Mira when they moved into the house was still hanging from one of her oldest oaks. Falling leaves were collecting on the decaying wood. She smiled at the memory of a night, during Mira's high school years, when she heard some giggling in the backyard and saw her passionately kissing a boy on the swing as they swayed back and forth. She had thought about having it removed, but she kind of liked things as they were. For now.

～

As she had hoped when she accepted the invitation, the deciduous-heavy mountains were saturated with Fall colors by the time she drove up the New York Thruway in mid-October. Even though Vassar was a stone's throw from the long declining, blue-collar Hudson River town of Poughkeepsie, it may as well have been in a different galaxy. Manhattan's exclusive private schools had been sending their budding artists, actors, and writers to Vassar for decades. It was the sort of campus where you might see productions of *Lysistrata* and *A Streetcar Named Desire* in the same night. The entire campus was chock full of breathtaking structures but Thompson Memorial Library was the *piece de resistance*. It was an intimidating grand Gothic building that resembled an English castle. Marian couldn't wait to tour the library and drink in the atmosphere. She always made it her duty to visit the great libraries of every city or university she visited. She thought it was kind of unfortunate Thompson was tucked away in upstate New York where millions of New Yorkers would never experience it.

Marian was directed to a parking lot and made her way to stately Rockefeller Hall where the conference was being held. Rockefeller Hall was an imposing hundred-year-old building that mixed Tudor and Elizabethan styles. Marian was gazing around when she was almost immediately flagged by one of the conference organizers, an amiable looking, portly man in his mid-40s, sporting a thickish rust-colored beard. His sweaty thick hand swallowed up Marian's as he shook hers vigorously.

"Thank you for coming Ms. Collingswood."

"Marian is fine. Professor Davis, I presume?" She gestured at the name tag pinned to his tweed jacket.

"Yes. Yes, I'm Paul Davis. Please call me Paul. We're very excited you could come. Take a walk with me so I can introduce you to some of our students and faculty."

Marian spent the rest of the morning speaking with the other faculty members and a bevy of very eager, mostly female, students. Marian was pleased that the students were certainly more diverse than when she went to school. Every time she spoke to another fresh-faced student, she pictured Mira. Marian understood when she had Mira that every time her daughter passed another milestone, it would bring her closer to being *ancient* like her parents. But since Mira had been gone for so long, she stopped receiving frequent reminders of just how much time was passing. Standing in front of so many young people today forced her to consider she was nearly a *half century* older than the students. *A half century?* How could that be? She felt like college was a few years ago.

By the time she was scheduled to speak in the late afternoon, her nerves, such as they were, had dissipated. She had a few glasses of wine with lunch which contributed to the easing of her stress level. Marian reminded herself that she had spoken to large crowds many times before. In her speech, she shared details of her life as a writer that she considered pertinent to undergraduate students exploring their way. She also read half a dozen poems drawn from her poetry collections during her time in front of the attendees. In the end, she received a warm reception which she hoped was sincere and not merely polite. Paul Davis stood to the side of her and beamed nearly the entire time she spoke. The look on his face suggested he was a real devotee which made her feel relevant in a way she hadn't felt in a long time. Charles shared some kind comments about her writing, but she didn't think he truly grasped the point of what she wrote. The poems didn't seem to contain much meaning to him.

When she finished, an animated Paul Davis shook her hand, strenuously again and leaned over and told her, "You are the star of the day. At least, in my humble opinion."

Marian thanked him, and he added he was looking forward to speaking with her at dinner at Alumnae House, where she was staying for the night. Marian made her way to Alumnae House, a nearly hundred-year-old charming inn that housed university guests and held dinners. Marian only had a little more than an hour to relax until the reception. In her cozy room, she kicked off her shoes and dropped back into one of the easy chairs in front of the cherry wood casement windows that covered one of the walls and quickly dozed off. She was suddenly back on the cruise ship frantically running around the halls searching for Nathan. The ship seemed to be empty and she couldn't seem to remember which room they were in. She was calling his name and ran upstairs to the top deck of the ship. She saw someone lying on a chaise lounge chair by the pool, but couldn't make out who it was since his back was to her. She ran over to the chair and stopped. The man turned and she was surprised to see it was Charles. He leaned over and offered his hand. Marian immediately asked were Nathan was.

Suddenly, she woke up discombobulated until she realized she was at Vassar. She checked her watch and saw she had been sleeping for almost an hour. She showered quickly and changed into a dress. She thought about not putting on makeup but then decided to put on some eye liner and blush. On the way down to the dining room, she tried to remember her dream, but all she could recall was that Nathan must have been in it since she was calling his name for some reason.

Paul Davis had arranged for her to sit with a few students he thought were particularly gifted and a few professors that taught poetry. He taught 19th century American literature, but he was there acting as a master of ceremonies as well. The conversation was spirited as they discussed what the role of poetry could be in a modern world. The students insisted poetry was driving popular music through rap and having a substantial impact on young people. Marian had to admit she hadn't really thought through their proposition having never really listened to rap music, but, in her day, Bob Dylan and other Folk musicians had adopted poetry to drive the national conversation on a host of social issues in their own way, of course. She was having such a good time she didn't realize that she had consumed several glasses of wine. By the end of the dinner she could feel her skin heat up and she was sure her cheeks were rosy red by now. Instant make-up. Paul Davis was clearly very pleased with himself for having arranged such an enlightening dinner. As the students bade their goodbyes, she turned to him.

"I think I need some air. Would you care to join me?"

"Sure."

Marian got up and realized she was a little woozy. Night had fallen and the October air felt good on her warm cheeks.

"Are you enjoying yourself?" Paul Davis asked.

"More than I expected."

"I'm glad. I thought you might. Or at least I hoped you would. Our students tend to be engaging, even a bit precocious."

"Have we met before?"

"Not properly, but I have attended a few of your book signings over the years. You might have signed a few of those books." A mischievous smile formed on his face.

"Well, I hope I was nice to you."

"Of course, you were."

"It's a funny thing emerging from years of solitude writing my poems and then facing people in these bookstores. Have you connected with them? Are they disappointed?"

"I can see that."

Before she could react, he leaned in to kiss her and pulled her close so that their bodies were nearly touching. Her head was still spinning from the wine, and at that moment, she felt like she could have kept on kissing him. After what seemed like a long time, she pulled back and waited for him to say something.

"Well. That was...*nice*."

"Yes. Yes, it was. I think I may have to lay down and sleep this off. It's been quite some time since I've had this much to drink. But thanks for a lovely evening."

Marian was reliving the kiss as she talked and could feel his beard against her face.

"Well, if you still want to have a nightcap you have my number."

"Can I ask you a question?"

"Am I married? No. Divorced."

"No. It wasn't that. But that's good to know. No, I was wondering what you see in me. You're probably twenty years younger than me?"

"Anyone who can write what you do…you know what I mean?"

Marian nodded and leaned in and kissed him on the cheek. That beard again.

"Thank you. In another lifetime."

"Good night Marian."

Marian pulled herself together and found her room and was somehow able to slide the key card into the slot to open the door. The door slammed behind her and she kicked off her heels and went to the bathroom and splashed water on her face. She felt her skin where his beard had rubbed and then walked over to the mirror in the bathroom. She looked at herself for a good long while. She started laughing and then couldn't stop.

41

janet

Marian stood in the drugstore and stared at the brightly colored wall of cards. She was pretty sure they weren't going to have one for a ninety first birthday, but she searched anyway. Weren't people living longer these days? Hadn't the card companies become hip to that fact? All she could find was an eightieth birthday card. She always felt a little guilty buying one of these cards, given she was supposed to be a writer of some note. But she wasn't going to write a poem for everyone's birthday, the expectations were too high. She leafed through the *Mother* cards and tried to find one that wasn't too intimate or artificially cheerful. She found one that straddled the line and made her way to the assisted living facility.

When she arrived at the front desk of the main house, she expected to be told her mother was busy with some activity. Her mother had become the de facto arts and crafts counselor, which was amusing to Marian because her mother struggled to help her in grade school with even the simplest projects. But she was told that her mother was in her room.

"Is she okay?"

"Physically, she's fine. For a 91-year-old. She has seemed down lately though. I'm sure seeing you will cheer her up."

"Because of her birthday?"

"She seemed okay at lunch when we sang happy birthday. But she didn't eat any cake and Janet loves her sweets."

"She does."

Marian walked to the part of the facility to which her mother had recently *graduated* to, where they had around the clock care as needed. Most of the people in this section were women who were confined to beds and chairs. She forced herself to smile at each of them as she walked by. She knew that one day one of those women might be her. Not a pleasant thought. Her mother's door was open and she was sitting in a chair sleeping soundly. Marian quietly walked over to her bed and sat down. She could see that her mother had placed her birthday party hat on the dresser next to an uneaten slice of cake. Nearby was a framed picture of her and Nathan from one of their trips to Grand Rapids. She was trying to remember what trip it was when her mother awakened.

"Marian."

"Hi."

"You snuck in on me."

"I did. Happy Birthday."

Marian handed her the card and her mother's favorite dark chocolate. Her mother had a little trouble opening the envelope, but finally managed to pry it open.

"Thank you."

"Your welcome. Cake looks good." Marian looked over at the dresser.

"I wasn't hungry."

"So, I hear."

"Everyone knows your business in this place."

"That means they care."

"So where were you last week?"

"I told you I was going to Florida."

"Never liked it there. You went with that man?"

"Charles. Yes."

"I miss him."

"Charles?"

"Nathan."

Marian had thought her mother would shrivel up and die here on the East Coast away from her church and her friends. Nathan had convinced Marian that her mother was a survivor and would eventually find her place in whatever community they found for her. He had been right and they had bonded once she moved closer to them. When Nathan died, it had taken all her courage to tell her mother. To Marian's surprise, a nurse had to give her mother oxygen and, eventually, a sleeping pill.

"I know you do. So do I."

"He was like a son."

"He felt the same way about you."

"As soon as I saw him get out of that rusty old car, I knew there was something special about him."

"He loved that piece of junk."

"You going to marry that man?"

"Charles? No one is asking me to get married mom."

"Man like that. Lost his wife. Don't be surprised."

"I'm not going to argue with you."

"Not on my birthday." Her mother smiled for the first time since she arrived.

"Exactly."

"Do you love him?"

"He's a good man."

Marian suddenly realized that her mother sounded exactly like her when she was interrogating Hilary about Roland. Had she fallen through some widow's trap door? Her mother was kind enough to avoid asking the unanswered query again.

"Am I going to see that baby of yours?"

"Of course, you will."

"She better hurry up."

"Why are you talking like that?"

"Do you know a lot of ninety-two-year olds?"

"Mom."

"What's she doing out in Seattle anyway? Tell her to come home."

"Did I come home?"

"Give me that cake."

She gave her mother the cake and fished around for a napkin or paper towel but couldn't find any. She walked into the hallway and then down to a desk with caregivers. One of them handed her some napkins, and by the time she made it back to the room, her mother had finished the cake and had nodded off holding the empty plate. There was some blue icing on her cheek, and she took a napkin and gently wiped it off. Her mother woke up for a few seconds and then nodded off again. Marian had been so caught up with Charles and Mira in recent months that she hadn't really taken stock of her mother's trajectory. She was no longer unofficial arts and crafts director anymore. She was fading and her mother was not unaware of it. Marian had always thought of herself as sandwiched in a protective cocoon between her mother and her daughter. She didn't know if she was prepared yet to be on the leading edge of the line.

42

parlor tricks

Marian glanced up at the audience such as it was. The bookstore was about ten miles from her house, and perhaps twenty hardy souls had sacrificed their Wednesday evening to listen to her. It was one of her favorite bookstores in the area which is why she agreed to speak. It was organized so that you could find the more interesting current books of the day near the entrance. As you moved deeper into the store, the shelves, teeming with used books, had a ramshackle appearance, but Marian enjoyed rummaging through the stacks. She thought maybe some people she knew from her town would come, but she didn't see any familiar faces. Just as well. The owner couldn't have been more than thirty and was evidently unaware he couldn't grow a respectable beard. His cheeks barely had enough wisps of hair to cover half the required area. In their conversations, he seemed sweet though and professed to have read some of her previous works. She doubted he had slogged through many of them, but was grateful someone his age was even cognizant of poetry.

Charles had taken a seat all the way in the back and clearly looked out of place. Maybe because she was the only person he knew. He was dressed like he was going to the opera and not a neighborhood bookstore. Marian had laughed when he pulled up at her house. She knew then he would stick out like a dandelion on an otherwise manicured lawn.

"What?"

"We're not going to see Rigoletto."

"Hey, it's not every day my gal gives a public performance."

"It's a bookstore. Lots of dust."

They got in the car, and she saw he was wearing shiny shoes.

"It may be old hat to you, but I've never been to a reading by a prominent author."

He patted her leg and grinned. She rolled her eyes.

"Very nice. Don't ask any questions or I'm going home in a cab."

"My lips are zipped. Quiet as a church mouse. Whatever that means."

"Good. They're all going to think you're my agent in that monkey suit anyhow."

The young man with the desperate beard introduced Marian and held up her new book. She thanked him and talked about the inspiration for the book. She thought she accomplished that without being too personal or maudlin given the subject matter. She had chosen the final poem in her book to read first.

Ribbons of light
narrowly peeked through
the drawn blinds
as dust settled
everywhere and
the threadbare apartment
was drained of all color
The angel descended
upon this place
while the dying lady
dreamed in the next room
of her mother brushing her hair
surprised
when she felt the angel
instead of her mother
so, the dying lady spoke in the
voice of a child:
"Where is my mother?"
there was no reply but
the angel took her hand
and she could see the angel
now wore her mother's face
the dying lady smiled
and she watched as the angel
cradled her heart

Marian looked up, and she could see Charles realized the inspiration for the poem because he was staring intently at his shoes to avoid eye contact. But Marian couldn't focus on him right now. She read three more poems from the collection and then took questions from the audience. Marian was always surprised when someone referenced a poem she had written in the past. Each question transported her back in time, so when the questions ceased she felt as if she had skipped across the surface of her life. She thanked the owner of the bookstore and walked outside with Charles. He opened the car door silently. She could see he was deep in thought. As soon he began to drive, he started talking.

"Do you believe in a higher power?"

"God?"

"God. Something else, maybe."

"I'd like to."

"But you don't?"

"Not really. Do you?"

"I do. I think Isabelle *is* with the angels."

"And Nathalie?"

"Yes. Of course."

"You don't go to church, though."

Marian wondered if that sounded too accusatory but, in her experience, those who were more religiously inclined also went to church regularly. Or, other houses of worship.

"I should go more."

"Why?"

"To be closer to God. Would you go with me?"

Marian paused. She hadn't been to church since Nathan's funeral, and she had no desire to return.

"I don't think so."

"Why not?"

"If I have a religion, it's probably my writing."

"I can see that. These people tonight were your disciples."

"The church of Marian. All are welcome. Saints and sinners. Sinners and readers preferred."

"I have to say I was a little envious tonight."

"You were?"

"Your gift moves people. As far as I'm concerned, God is talking through you to these people. Don't you see that?"

"I don't know. I would say that I am more of a magician who is performing parlor tricks. Certainly, not a deity."

"Magicians don't touch peoples' souls."

"I get your point. It's not something I take lightly, but there is a selfish aspect to what I do. There is an element of *here I am*. You know what I mean?"

"I think I understand what you're saying, but I want to change the subject for a minute."

"To something heavier?" Marian smiled.

"I want to come with you."

"To?"

"To Seattle. When Mira has the baby."

"Oh. I see."

"Is that a no?"

"No, that's not a no. I just assumed I was going alone."

"Why would you assume that?"

"I don't know. I guess you barely know her, so it didn't occur to me that you would want to go. I never thought otherwise. I know that sounded really cold and I didn't mean it to sound that way."

"She's your daughter, so it *interests* me."

"I know it does." Marian was backpedaling after her knee jerk reaction.

"If it's okay with her, of course."

"I'm sure she would like to get to know you." Marian wasn't entirely sure of that.

"Well, you should ask."

"Of course. I will."

"Good. So, it's settled?"

"Yes."

Marian thought back to her conversation with her mother. Maybe she was right after all. How long would he wait before asking her to get married? She envisioned herself in a wedding dress standing in some church, and all she could think was how ridiculous that might look. She actually didn't know how Mira would react to a virtual stranger ogling her newborn child. A stand-in for her father. She would have to call her tomorrow after Charles went home.

43

grandma

On the way to JFK airport, Marian's mind kept flashing to babies. She recalled Nathan had been elated and very animated when she told him she thought she was in labor. Marian wasn't due for almost three weeks and she wasn't prepared mentally to give birth so soon. She remembered when she was able to catch her breath between the excruciating contractions, she yelled at him to wipe the goofy grin off his face. To her exhausted self, it almost seemed sadistic. Marian had decided long ago she was not going to be outmaneuvered by that baby boy in Mira's womb, and she was going to go to Seattle at least a few weeks before the due date. She had spoken to Mira after Charles had expressed his desire to accompany her. She was a little surprised that Mira seemed completely unconcerned about having Charles rooting about with her in the hospital corridors in Seattle. Marian figured that, at this point, Mira just wanted her body back and probably couldn't focus on much else. Or she was just lying to her.

Charles had reserved one of those ostentatious stretch limousines for the ride to the airport. He assured her that it wasn't much more than a regular taxi since his old company had an arrangement that went back many years. There was so much unused space she felt as if she was Jonah and that they had been swallowed whole. Charles kept nervously tapping her hand, and Marian wanted him to stop but didn't say anything. She could see they were in Queens now and wondered exactly where they were relative to Martin's old apartment. She had been surprised to see him at Nathan's funeral. She knew Nathan had still been in touch with him, but she couldn't find his number in Nathan's papers. Martin had tears in his eyes when they hugged and held her close for more than a few moments. She wasn't even sure why she had been happy to see him, since he was a reminder of the darkest chapter of their marriage. In the end, she decided it was probably because she knew how fond he was of Nathan and how when Nathan needed him, he was there. On that particular day, that resonated with her. Now that they were driving beneath the elevated train, she knew it wouldn't be long before they reached the airport. She wasn't sure when it started, but there was a voice in her head that was growing louder, and today she wasn't sure she could ignore it anymore. When the limousine turned towards the *Departing Flights* sign she began to notice her breathing. The car pulled up in front of the curb and her heart was pounding. As Charles was about to open the door, she stopped him.

"Wait."

"What's wrong? You look pale."

"I want to go alone."

"Now you tell me this? Is this Mira talking?"

"No."

"What am I missing?"

The driver interrupted and said he was getting their luggage.

"I keep trying to picture you there. In the hospital. With us. I just think it would be better if I did this myself."

The driver tapped the window.

"Give us a minute!" Charles barked.

"You're sure about this?"

"I am."

Her blood was pumping so fast she felt like her whole head was going to twist off. Charles kept staring at her like she was one of his children who had just misbehaved.

"Are we done?" he finally asked.

The driver opened the door and implored them to step out. Marian leaned over and kissed Charles on the cheek and walked out of the car.

"I'll call you when I get there." Marian said, although she said it so quietly, she wasn't sure if she actually said it.

~

"You seriously left him in the limo at the airport?"

Marian was embarrassed, but she had to confess her less than stellar behavior so she could begin to understand it herself.

"Yes. I know it was horrible of me."

"Well, it took some guts, that's for sure. So, he just turned around and went home in the limo?"

"I suppose so."

"Wow. That's… so unlike you!"

"You don't have to rub it in. Look how big you got."

"I'm ready to explode. This kid needs to evacuate."

Mira patted her abdomen and tried to figure out a way to make the seatbelt in the back of the taxi cover her torso without making her uncomfortable.

"So, are you going to break up with him, or was that *it*?"

"I don't know. I can't imagine he'll get over this. I'm not sure I would."

"Are you going to call him?"

"I think I told him I would."

"I thought you were happy with him?"

"He's a very nice man. I don't have any major complaints, really. I don't think I want a constant companion. You know what I mean?"

"What *do* you want?"

"Right now, I want to be a grandmother. I don't think I want to share that with anyone."

"But, I'm out *here*."

"Maybe I'll move."

"Really?"

"Maybe not for a little while. Someday."

"Are you sure about all this? You're going to be all alone in that big house."

"Alone with my favorite person." Marian smiled.

"Mine too."

Marian slowly placed her hand on Mira's protruding belly and waited. After a moment, she felt the baby move and they smiled at each other. It wouldn't be long now.

about the author

Ken Levine was born in Brooklyn, New York. He is currently a resident of Allendale, New Jersey and is married and raising his three children. He is employed as the Deputy Managing Counsel for the United States Postal Service's Northeast Area. This is his third novel.

His first was *North of Nowhere* and his second was *Before it Gets Dark*.

Made in the USA
Coppell, TX
26 May 2023